SORRY TO DISRUPT THE PEACE

PATRICK COTTRELL

McSWEENEY'S
SAN FRANCISCO

McSWEENEY'S
SAN FRANCISCO

Cover design and illustration by Sunra Thompson

Printed in the United States.

ISBN: 978-1-963270-64-8

10 9 8 7 6 5 4 3

www.mcsweeneys.net

WINNER OF THE 2017 BARNES AND NOBLE
DISCOVER GREAT NEW WRITERS AWARD FOR FICTION

WINNER OF A 2018 WHITING AWARD FOR FICTION

2017 WINNER OF INDEPENDENT PUBLISHER BOOK AWARDS
GOLD MEDAL FOR FIRST FICTION

ONE OF BUZZFEED'S, VULTURE'S, *NYLON*'S, AND LITHUB'S
MOST ANTICIPATED BOOKS OF 2017

ONE OF ELECTRIC LITERATURE'S, LARGEHEARTED BOY'S,
AND ENTROPY'S BEST BOOKS OF 2017

"A strange and lovely thing. Cottrell fills every page with an impossible-to-ignore voice, characterized by its idiosyncrasies and intelligence." —Ilana Masad, *San Francisco Chronicle*

"Patrick Cottrell's remarkable debut possesses something of the deadpan strangeness of Jane Bowles's *Two Serious Ladies*, yet the book is electrifying in its freshness. A sort of existential detective hunt—equal parts hilarious and heartbreaking."

—Lucy Scholes, *The Guardian*

"Comic and unsettling. Cottrell's writing lacks the solemnity we might expect from a novel about suicide. And this is what is so striking about *Sorry to Disrupt the Peace*. It is not dominated by the death that has occurred; instead, it is an exploration of the absurd, the contradictory and the human. Much like the acerbic tone of the novels' title, Cottrell's narrator bristles with defiance."

——Alex Howlett, *Times Literary Supplement*

"A sort of Korean-American noir, lean and wry and darkly compelling, I respectfully suggest you read him now."

—Ed Park, author of *Personal Days*

"Patrick Cottrell's prose does so many of my favorite things—some too subtle to talk about without spoiling, but one thing I have to mention is the way in which his heroine's investigation of a suicide draws the reader right into the heart of this wonderfully spiky hedgehog of a book and then elbows us yet further along into what is ultimately a tremendously moving act of imagination."

—Helen Oyeyemi, author of *A New New Me*

"Patrick Cottrell's adoption of the rambling and specific absurd will and must delight. This is a graceful claim not just about writing but about a way of being in the world, an always new and necessary way to contend with this garbage that surrounds us, these false portraits of our hearts and minds. This book is not a diversion—it's a lifeline."

—Jesse Ball, author of *The Repeat Room*

"*Sorry to Disrupt the Peace* had me opening my mouth to laugh only to feel sobs come tumbling out. It's absurd, feeling so much at once, but it's a distinctly human absurdity that Patrick Cottrell has masterfully created in this book. In the end I felt ebullient and spent, grateful to be reminded that life is only funny and gorgeous because life is also strange and sad."

—Lindsay Hunter, author of *Hot Springs Drive*

"'Behind every suicide, there is a door.' So says Helen, aka Sister Reliability, aka 'spinster from a book,' who is determined to open the door behind her adoptive brother's recent death. Her search takes her from a studio apartment in NYC to a childhood home in Milwaukee, and yet the investigation is as philosophical as it is practical, as was, perhaps, the death itself. Patrick Cottrell's *Sorry to Disrupt the Peace* is a beguiling debut: absurdly funny, surprisingly beautiful, and ultimately sad as fuck."

—Danielle Dutton, author of *Margaret the First*

"In this completely absorbing novel of devastation and estrangement, Patrick Cottrell introduces himself as a modern Robert Walser. His voice is unflinching, unforgettable, and animated with a restless sense of humor."

—Catherine Lacey, author of *The Möbius Book*

"Disturbing and hilarious, Cottrell's haunting debut explores the toxic fumes that radiate from the narrator's dysfunctional familial network, arresting development, truncating lives, and dragging everything into a vertiginous chasm the narrator, Helen Moran, investigates. Cottrell seduces his readers into an uncanny abyss.

—Azareen Van der Vliet Oloomi, author of *Call Me Zebra*, winner of the PEN/Faulkner Award

"Helen's foggy view of reality is a dark, dark comedic well, and debut novelist Cottrell tells his story with gutsy style, glowing sentences, and true feeling." —Annie Bostrom, *Booklist*

"In Cottrell's stellar debut novel, 32-year-old Helen is in her Manhattan apartment when she receives a call that her adoptive brother has killed himself... The real attraction here is Helen: her perspective ranges from sharp (New York is 'a city so rich it funds poetry') to askew ('People who call themselves photographers are fake... the real charlatans of our time. Behind a photo is a perfectly fake person, scrubbed of all flaws, dead inside') to unhinged (her adoptive parents' grieving takes the physical form of a middle-aged European man who walks around the house and helps himself to pizza). Cottrell gives Helen the impossible task of understanding what would drive another person to suicide, and the result is complex and mysterious, yet, in the end, deeply human and empathetic."

—*Publishers Weekly* (starred)

"*Sorry to Disrupt the Peace* is a book you can't put down, and once you do, the whole world shifts." —Erynn Porter, *Electric Literature*

For Kevin

1

SEPTEMBER 30TH, THE DAY I RECEIVED the news of my adoptive brother's death, I also received a brand-new couch from IKEA. To clarify, I was the only one who happened to be physically present the day my roommate Julie's brand-new couch arrived at our shared studio apartment in Manhattan. That day my phone did not stop ringing because my roommate Julie listed my phone number as the main contact for the furniture-delivery company instead of her own. The delivery driver called multiple times because he could not find the apartment building. There was a mix-up on the invoice or the address of the apartment had been smudged into a black thumbprint, also, at the time, a large green trash receptacle the size of a dump truck was placed in front of the building, which blocked the view of the numbers above the front door.

It's strange, I said to the driver on the phone, it's as if there are all these unseen forces out in the world actively working against us.

What do you mean? said the driver. Listen ma'am, I'm just trying to deliver a couch.

By the time the delivery driver had located the building, by the time the couch had been delivered, unpacked, and assembled, by the time multiple forms on a clipboard had been signed and shuffled away, I was so physically drained, I collapsed onto my roommate Julie's brand-new piece of furniture and proceeded to sweat into the leather cushions and I nearly threw up from the stench of the cowhide mingling with the scent of my own sweat. As soon as I collapsed and sweated onto the couch and felt nauseous, my phone, somewhere across the apartment, began to ring again. I ignored it for a moment, unsure if I would be able to stand up. I was shocked by how large the couch was, how it nearly swallowed up my roommate Julie's entire side of the apartment. When I finally stood up and located my phone behind an empty box, I was surprised to hear a rough and masculine voice, a voice that had traveled across deserts, a voice that had swallowed up countless scrolls of sandpaper and parchment.

Is this Helen? It's your Uncle Geoff.

Uncle Geoff, what a surprise, I said pleasantly. I thought you refused to own a phone. I laughed a slight and friendly laugh. Wasn't that your quirky thing, to refuse to own a phone?

The voice let out a sigh. Your mother wanted me to talk to you. To tell you what happened.

Go on, I'm listening.

The voice broke out into sobs.

What? I can't understand you.

A few seconds passed as the voice attempted to control itself.

He's gone, said the voice. Your mother wanted me to tell you.

Who? I said. And what do you mean by gone, exactly?

...

...

Your brother died last night, he said.

I was looking at the row of boxes that the brand-new couch and its pillows had arrived in, the boxes that the furniture-delivery company did not bother to break down and recycle because they were running late, the now-empty boxes I had arranged so neatly, stacked directly across from the brand-new couch. I had cut off the flaps with an X-acto knife and I was now staring at the flat and even sides as my brain attempted to absorb the information.

He died? I said. Was he sick? What are you talking about? No one told me he was sick!

The voice on the other line stopped speaking and started to wail and it sounded like a thousand rusty needle tips scratching across an endless sheet of metal. As soon as I heard it, I was confident the sound would haunt me for the rest of my life.

It was unexpected. He died unexpectedly.

What is that supposed to mean? That means nothing to me!

It means he took his own life, said the voice.

The boxes I had placed so neatly across from the couch moved closer to my eyes, closer to my brain, and then they melted into a smooth and flat box-colored screen. The needle-scratching sound started up again.

Where are they? I shouted to try to get the sound to stop.

Who? Where's who?

My adoptive parents!

They're at their house. I'll call you later with the funeral arrangements, if you decide to come.

What kind of funeral? I said. Is it a Catholic one?

I'm not sure, said the voice, slightly wavering. No one's going to force you to come, if you have other things you need to do. Whatever you want. It's up to you.

He hung up on me and the wailing sound went away, but the needle-scraping sound stayed with me, chilling me to the bone. Stop your scraping! I screamed to no one. I plugged my ears with the foam peanuts left over from the boxes and the sound of my breathing drowned out the scraping. I sat down on the floor and pulled off the pillows from the brand-new couch and propped them up behind my back. A Catholic funeral, I thought to myself, he would have hated that; he only went to church to appease our adoptive parents, he didn't really believe in religion, he didn't believe in anything like that. I turned around and allowed myself to begin sobbing into my roommate Julie's brand-new leather pillows to muffle the sounds I couldn't hear anyway, poor little adoptive brother, I sobbed. I must have sobbed for hours. As my sobbing ebbed, I began to search my mind for the cause of his life-taking. Were there clues? There must have been clues. There must have been clues and signs hiding all over the place, the place of his life.

I continued to come up with nothing except an image of his small brown Korean eyes that looked nothing like my Korean eyes, as we were each adopted from different biological families, and I remembered suddenly the last time I saw him, the time he had come all the way from Milwaukee to drop in on me in New York City, the time I tried to give him a hug, he had refused me, he had turned away sharply, muttering something about how he was sick with a bad cold and he didn't want to infect me. I remembered it was strange then, how he pulled away from me, his one and only adoptive sister. I want to hug you, you silly little man, I might have said. I might have pulled him close to me and hugged him anyway. I was always forcing people to do things they didn't want to do.

Twenty-nine years old and gone. I went back to my sobbing and then my sobbing turned into a percussive shaking and a small vase with plastic flowers fell off my roommate Julie's bookshelf, but it didn't shatter into pieces, it just rolled dumbly across the wooden floor. I began to worry my roommate Julie would walk in and see me staining her new pillows with the fluids of my grieving. The eye is a terrible organ, I thought as I glanced around the apartment for a box of tissues. It took me a while to compose myself. I have always moved at the speed of caves and mountains.

When I finished my mucous-ridden sobbing, I decided firmly that I, Helen Moran, would go to my childhood home in Milwaukee and be a supportive beam of light for my adoptive parents in their despair. You're the only one left; you will be the one, I decided, and I marched right up to the boxes and put my hands on them to steady myself. Yes, I will go to that house, I said to no one. I pictured in my mind the house at the bottom of the hill, a dark house I had not set foot inside for many years, a house as large and spacious as a medieval fortress, with enough square footage for at least one or two more Catholic families. It was not a cheaply built house, as my adoptive father liked to say. *It did not come cheaply built*. My parents are somewhat rich, but, like most Midwesterners, they are the cheapest people I have ever known. Despite their lack of financial stress, they are extravagant in their cheapness, their discount-hunting, their coupon-scissoring, their manuals on how to save. It was important, they said, to think about the catastrophic future, to always have a backup account filled with hundreds of thousands of dollars. To think about it too much depressed me. My entire existence was infected by this cheapness, this so-called frugality. Of course, it would be wrong not to acknowledge that these values of cheapness or frugality were what allowed once-orphans like myself and my now-dead adoptive brother to grow up, and to thrive even, in the comfort and security of the not cheaply built house. But there would be no more thriving for us, as one of us was dead.

My brain was working very hard inside the housing of its skull. Was it surprising they themselves didn't call me? We hadn't talked in months, so perhaps not. I wasn't even that upset they didn't call; I preferred not to talk on the phone, especially under awkward and distressing circumstances. What else could a human being do in this situation? I wondered. When I received the phone call informing me of my adoptive brother's death, I knew it was imperative that I return to the Catholic fortress, I had no choice but to offer a helping hand to my shell-shocked adoptive parents during what must be a time of severe physical exhaustion and emotional anguish, despite the distance presently between us.

At your service, I imagined myself saying as I bowed to them, like a humble servant. Then I would envelop them in the warmth of my charity and my supportive beam of light. I am a helpfulness virtuoso and it is time to take my talents to my childhood home, I would have to tell my roommate Julie. That's how it will go, I said to myself. But then, throughout that time of saying to myself how it would go, it dawned upon me: how can I, Helen Moran, help my poor adoptive parents withstand the death of my adoptive brother when I understand nothing regarding the circumstances of the death itself?

I was curious about the abyss. The abyss, round and dark as a child's mouth. How did he die? I wondered. Was it in a violent manner? Uncle Geoff didn't specify. Was Uncle Geoff even my uncle at all? Or was he my adoptive mother's cousin? Then the image of the abyss began to take hold of my thoughts and suddenly, I could not stop thinking about it and saying things to myself as I stood in my shared studio apartment in Manhattan propping my body up against the boxes.

I said to myself: I'll just go have a quick look-see, I'll just stand in the middle of the house and look around, still as a statue, a quick little look is all I will take. The more I thought about it, the more invested I became in finding out what happened to my adoptive brother, because whatever happened to him was surely very odd. I believed that. When a human being takes his or her own life, the circumstances are always very odd and serious and they must be looked into. It must be done with the rigor of a proper metaphysical investigation. Perhaps to investigate his death would revitalize my own life, and if I could communicate my eventual findings to them, it would strengthen and support the lives of my adoptive parents as well. I began to feel rational and purposeful. It's unnatural to not want to be alive anymore, I said to myself. *Life itself is the instinct for growth, for survival,*
for an accumulation of forces… That's what Nietzsche said, phi- 1
losopher of life!

I kept propping myself up in front of the boxes and saying more and more things to no one. I will look thoroughly around the house, I said, an investigation virtuoso, leaving no room unturned, because a thorough and professional investigation of the house is precisely what the situation calls for. I pictured it in my mind: I walk up to the door of my childhood home, a door painted black with a brass kick plate, and ring the doorbell. My adoptive parents open the door and greet me warmly with a plate of cookies and skim milk or day-old muffins and lukewarm tea. I saw us setting aside our various issues and presenting to the world a unified front, I saw us braiding our grief into a rope, a strong and shiny rope we would take out and show people who asked us what it was like to lose someone to suicide.

I would have to examine every fiber of his bedroom with a magnifying glass. It was simple, I could see. Of course I would have to begin there. When he was living, my adoptive brother lived off and on with our adoptive parents for most of his twenty-nine years on the planet. In fact, he spent more than three-quarters of his life in his childhood bedroom, if you included sleeping. There was information there in the house, in the bedroom and in the closet. The closet would contain the most information, I said to no one, that disgusting closet that accumulated piles and piles of clothes, books, broken vases, empty picture frames, batteries, suitcases, pieces of garbage, broken computers, little jars with baby teeth. The insides of my nose started to burn because even though I was approximately nine hundred miles away from my adoptive brother's closet in suburban Milwaukee, situated as I was upright with my hands on the boxes in my shared studio apartment in Manhattan, somehow the smell of the closet in Milwaukee wafted up through my nostrils and got stuck inside my nasal cavities and caused the passages to burn. I recognized that burning, that sulfurous stench as the singular property of the closet: its dead-animal odor. Because a small animal settled in between the walls and died in there, behind the closet. Because it took my adoptive mother an entire summer to figure out what the smell was and to call pest-control services. They had a terrible time removing it, they were only able to remove pieces of the dead animal with the aid of a small and specialized scraping device from China. The other dead-animal parts had already been absorbed into the rotting wood and there they remained, they were there causing that sulfurous stench long after I moved out of the house, and long after I left Milwaukee to begin my life in New York City.

It made me laugh a little, the idea of going about my business, my metaphysical investigations, in the middle of this familial nightmare. Helen Moran, are you mad? I should have asked myself. Helen Moran, I should have cried out, *are you an insane monster*? The truth is, I would only have laughed or coughed into my hands or averted my eyes because I could not think of anything else to do, not a single thing. The idea of the investigation had already taken root inside my brain. A little self-knowledge can be a very productive thing, I said to no one. I am a very productive person, I said as I opened the windows of my shared studio apartment. I shouted things to the passersby on the crummy sidewalks below. I can be a very helpful person! I screamed. A woman pushing a double-wide stroller looked up at me with concern. At your service, bitches! I shouted. I saluted the pigeons and the rats. I said to no one, What you are doing, Helen, is not only very ethical, it is what is required.

2

AT THE TIME OF HIS DEATH I was a thirty-two-year-old woman, single, childless, irregularly menstruating, college-educated, and partially employed. If I looked in the mirror, I saw something upright and plain. Or perhaps hunched over and plain, it depended. Long, long ago I made peace with my plainness. I made peace with piano lessons that went nowhere because I had no natural talent or aptitude for music. I made peace with the coarse black hair that grows out of my head and hangs down stiffly to my shoulders. One day I even made peace with my uterus. Living in New York City for five years, I had discovered the easiest way to distinguish oneself was to have a conscience or a sense of morality, since most people in Manhattan were extraordinary thieves of various standing, some of them multi-billionaires. Over time, I became a genius at being ethical, I discovered that it was *my true calling*. I made little to no money as a part-time after-school supervisor of troubled young people, with the side work of ordering paper products for the toilets. After my first week, the troubled people gave me a nickname.

Hey, Sister Reliability, what's up? Bum me a cigarette. Suck my dick. They never stopped smoking or saying disgusting things to me, those troubled young people living and dying in Manhattan, sewer of the earth! I was living and dying right next to them all the while attempting to maintain an ethical stance as their supervisor, although some days I will admit it was difficult to tell who was supervising whom.

In theory, I have always been interested in the idea of ethical practices: how to live, what to do, so to speak. Being interested in something is partially how I cultivated my talent and genius, I thought, because I wasn't born this way, I was born instead with no natural talents or capacities, I was born as a shabby little baby, but after a long and unremarkable time, I *became* a virtuous woman, I transformed myself into something *good*, and one by-product of this particular nature was behavior that seemed to land mostly on the ethical side of things and, at worst, the retiring and overly apologetic side. Pragmatic, I have always preferred to be in the background, unobserved; I preferred to play the role of the detached observer / receiver, the way one would live if one lived and spoke and shat inside a puffy white cloud floating along above the world harmlessly like a balloon.

Think of me as your balloon, I would tell my troubled young people, I'm always next to you or hovering right above you. After

I said that, I noticed some of them didn't seem to know what a balloon was, they looked at me so confusedly, I was compelled to assume they had never even seen a fucking balloon. So one bright afternoon a few months ago, I drank a few gin-and-tonics before work, which I do not often do, and then I forced them to watch a DVD of *The Red Balloon* at our after-school facility. We were not allowed to sit alone in darkened rooms with the troubled young people, all of the overhead lights were on, making it difficult to see the screen. My face was bright red, like the balloon, which one of them observed astutely. I told them to focus on the beautiful film I was screening for their viewing pleasure and to stop looking at me. Then I broke the rules and turned off the lights. I spent the next five minutes or so pointing out for them how each scene was so artfully composed, it was almost like watching a painting come alive.

It's a painting come alive, children, do you see it? I said with excitement.

Halfway through the film, I felt nauseous, ran into the bathroom, locked the door, and threw up for almost an hour. When I came out, the lights were on, the movie shut off, and they sat there in silence, staring at me with their mouths opened. I must have been making really loud retching sounds.

The point is I always knew my talents would be useful one day, I said to the coworker who asked me what I was doing showing a group of at-risk Latino and African American teenage boys *The Red Balloon*. Then I employed a strategy I have honed throughout my life when asked a difficult question: to respond with a question of my own. I asked my coworker pointedly what the troubled people's race had to do with it, couldn't Latino and African American people watch and enjoy *The Red Balloon*? And what I said previously was true: I always knew my talents would be helpful to someone, someday.

It took me the entire day after the phone call with Uncle Geoff to begin to clear my head. I wasn't feeling well in the first place; I had called in sick to work earlier that morning. I spent the rest of the day in bed sobbing, coughing, and toying with the idea of calling my adoptive parents. Surely they would call me, I thought. A call never came. My roommate Julie texted me to ask what the couch looked like, did it look good, could I take a picture of it for her as she would be spending the night at her boyfriend's place and wouldn't see it until tomorrow. And what was I supposed to say to that?

That night, somewhere in between my sobbing, somewhere in the middle of my hysteria, the seeds of a plan had germinated. I calmed and composed myself. I have always been a rational and relational person; I didn't recognize this hysterical, sobbing woman. No. I took care of my peace, I kept it in spotless condition. As the plan germinated, I pictured the funeral, that great spectacle of mourning. I saw strangers standing around taking part in a superficial grief performance ostensibly to both celebrate and mourn a dead person they never bothered to know when he was alive. The next morning, I woke up and saw without question what needed to be done. It was necessary that I attend the funeral, because I was the only one, perhaps, who once knew and understood him.

I stared at the white wall on my side of the studio apartment. A few days ago, when he was alive, I had wiped down all of the walls of my shared studio apartment with a can of cleaning disinfectant, then a rag soaked in lemon oil. Overnight, everything changed, temporally. Everything was now before and after his suicide. I was located in the after-phase.

It was my very observational acumen combined with a genius for ethical practices that compelled me to stuff my canvas suitcase with all of my clothes and to book a same-day plane ticket to my childhood home. Before I put the flight on my credit card, I spent an hour looking online at sweaters on sale, because I had nothing black to wear to the funeral. It took me a long time because there were so many different types of sweaters. *Why* were there so many different types of sweaters? Fluffy sweaters and mohair sweaters and fisherman sweaters and boyfriend sweaters. Which sweater should I order? I wondered. Finally, I chose a black turtleneck sweater, ribbed, half off. I was always thinking ahead and strategically planning. After I pressed CONFIRM SALE, I smacked my forehead. I should have had it delivered to my adoptive parents' address! It took a half hour on the phone waiting to speak to customer service to get the sweater sent to the right address. During this time of waiting, it began to dawn upon me that in fact this family tragedy had come at the worst possible time for me, as my work status was currently under probation, even so, there was no question as to whether I would go home or not. Once I reached an actual human, the sweater situation was straightened out almost immediately, but not before I explained to the customer-service agent the special purpose of the sweater: a funeral sweater for a suicide. She understood, and waived the cost for shipping. I hung up the phone and went back to my computer.

I booked the one-way plane ticket to Milwaukee, then began to compose an email to my supervisor. The subject line was A DEATH IN THE FAMILY (NOT THE BOOK). I wrote to him that there had been a death in my adoptive family. My adoptive family was reduced to ashes. Supervisor, you can't see me now, I typed, but I'm crying. It's like a sibling Hiroshima. One minute he was there, the next he's a shadow.

My leaving would be frowned upon, I knew. A few months ago, I was astonished to learn I was the subject of an internal investigation, which I snorted at with laughter because I was the most ethical person in the history of the organization, I let it be known regularly how upright my behavior was especially in contrast to my own supervisor, some kind of Adolf Eichmann type. He doesn't do anything except what he's told, I told anyone who would listen, he carries out his orders without thinking about the conditions of the troubled young people.

It's all about the bottom line with him, I said to anyone with ears, it's all about living on less and less. Less than gossamer and floss! I once said, only to realize I had been shouting.

Everyone needs toilet paper and tissues, I would say calmly as I put in my weekly orders, everyone needs paper towels and moist towelettes.

He could respond only with numbers and financial feasibility and so-called facts.

What are they supposed to do? I screamed at him a week ago. Wipe the shit off with the back of their hands? Then the shit gets spread all around and everything they touch has shit-traces!

There were a few exceptions to this tense relationality. Some of my troubled young people saw me as I really was, and eventually I went on to befriend them even after they left my supervision. I gave them my personal telephone number and home address in case they wanted to reach me outside of the facility, in case they wanted to grab lunch or go see a movie. And how was it that I was the only one who listened to the troubled people and treated them as peers instead of minions? And what would my troubled young people do while I was away in Milwaukee attending to my adoptive parents? I wondered. They would face hardship after hardship, certainly, especially without their cigarettes or their candy. Some of them would go through withdrawal and cravings. Absolutely they would suffer during my time away.

It couldn't have happened at a worse time, I said to myself as I printed out a plane ticket on my roommate Julie's printer. In fact it's audacious to leave at a time like this, especially when my work is under such intense scrutiny, but my adoptive family has left me with no choice. When faced with a crisis one is compelled to act in an ethical manner. And it cannot be ignored that this would be an excellent time to showcase my talents.

I'm the only one left, I typed to my supervisor, I'm buying a one-way ticket and I'm not sure when I will return. Sincerely, Sister Reliability, I signed it, because even though my supervisor did not call me Sister Reliability, even though he refused to call me Sister Reliability, the troubled young people certainly did, and it was mostly for their sake I was writing at all.

3

AFTER I PROOFREAD MY EMAIL for spelling and grammatical errors, I pressed send. Everyone loves to press send, I thought as I pictured the email swooping into my supervisor's inbox. Then I imagined myself swooping confidently into the Midwest as fierce as a swan to assist my adoptive parents. Time passed quickly or maybe it dissolved. Perhaps it shattered! I finished packing my canvas suitcase. I called a car. When tragedies occur, time slows down or speeds up. I could put forth theories about time to entertain myself, most of them superficial. That's the truth. I only knew time existed because as the years went on, my flesh slackened and my muscles ached. It was as if my bones were wearing some kind of flesh muumuu. Time itself is nothing but a construction to organize and measure flesh decay.

October 1st, somewhere between 24 and 48 hours after his death, approximately an hour before I boarded a direct, nonstop flight to Milwaukee, I drank six shots of espresso. The airport barista didn't want to give me six shots, she said it would make me sick, but I insisted. To make her feel better, I told her I would spit out some of it, and I did, I spit it out into a garbage can. My flight was on time, which made me feel calm and generous and philosophical, considering the wretched circumstances. I settled down into my assigned window seat and took out my traveler kit from the canvas suitcase, which I refused to check, and I swallowed a pill for sinus-pressure relief. After I stowed everything neatly under the seat in front of me, something inside me rumbled; it took me a minute to come to the realization that I needed to take a monstrous shit. I flew at once out of my seat, squeezed by all of the people crowding the aisle with their duffel bags and children, and shoved myself into the tiny bathroom, cramming my elbows into my stomach, hunched over, as the shit started to come out. For no reason at all, I thought of a horse and an apple cart, the horse pulling the little cart of bright red apples up a partially shaded gray hill. They had to knock on the door to get me to come out, the shit was so large and dense, it must have taken almost fifteen minutes to evacuate.

A stewardess roved up and down the aisle and made sure people's seatbelts were fastened. I slid the side of my ass against the knees of the two men sitting in my row. I sat down again. They did the yellow-cup mask demonstration, then the plane took off. I lifted the window shade and turned my attention to the view of the soot-covered buildings and assorted filth. I had succeeded in calming myself. For no reason, I began to feel better, I began to feel like a human again. When we reached the altitude of clouds, I distracted myself from my woeful and calamitous situation by reading a book, an LGBT novel about a man who transitions into a woman and then decides to go back to being a man. I liked stories about people changing their minds and undoing themselves, although in the case of de-transitioning, it's most likely a rare occurrence, and I had to question the writer's motives in portraying it. Setting aside the problematic parts of the book, I related deeply to the main character's challenges when it came to friendship. Because he had made trans-friendly allies during his transition, when he transitioned back into a cis-gendered man, he lost all of his friends. Stunned, I put the book down. There was an odd and haunting parallel to my own life and experiences. I always related any given situation back to myself, another one of my great talents, and I remembered how much difficulty I had leaving Milwaukee and all the troubled relations I left behind. Like the protagonist in the LGBT novel, I had once lost all my friends, in the year 2008. Friendship itself had always been difficult, as difficult as it is for anyone, I thought sitting on the plane. About five years ago, I was semi-famous in Milwaukee for a brief moment, I even received attention in the local newspaper. I referred to myself as an emerging artist, I made crumbling assemblages out of found objects, and innovative performance artists and sculptors and writers and independent film directors and producers surrounded me, and there was an art critic for the local weekly who could not stop writing about all of us. It was a beautiful time, people had art galleries in their attics, and every weekend there was a show to go to, or some kind of absurdist performance theater, where women took off their clothes, even ugly women with misshapen bodies like myself, and men swung around their erections like police batons, my once-friends! Afterward, all of these fashionable and intellectually advanced people, even the ugly ones, went to a bar with a two-lane bowling alley in the basement. No one seemed to care that anyone was ugly, it was beside the point. My fame was very limited to a specific group of people who lived downtown, no one in the suburbs cared about us. Not even my adoptive family knew about it, partially because they never read the weekly newspaper and partially because it was for such a brief time. For a time as brief as candles, people were drawn to me, people searched me out, they asked where I was if I wasn't there, some people even said I was mildly beautiful. Or perhaps they said I was beautifully mild. Either way. I was always very plain and somewhat shabby, no matter, there must have been an aura of artistic intensity around me, even though I didn't go to college for art, I went to college for a practical degree in English, you can do anything with an English degree, a guidance counselor told me. I fashioned myself as an artistic person, artistic in my way of living, artistic in my choice of clothing. My favorite shirt at the time was found in a garbage can at the intersection of Farwell and Pleasant, a turquoise sweatshirt with an appliqué of a dog and rabbit in a hot air balloon basket. The hot air balloon itself was pink suede. So it was no surprise that once, a very long time ago, some people gravitated toward me.

Then something went wrong, someone turned against me, perhaps out of jealousy, I'll never know, and he or she circulated a rumor that I was an artistic hack and called into question the originality of my work. It was said that my assemblages of found objects and texts owed too much to the work of Joseph Cornell and Henry Darger. A few weeks later an article appeared in the weekly newspaper with a photo of me and my work captioned:

Appropriation or theft: the failed work of Milwaukee's Helen Moran. It was an ugly scene; everywhere I went people whispered that I was a plagiarist and a fraud. A side-by-side comparison of my work to the works of Cornell and Darger showed certain similar technical flourishes and extensions, and although it was easy to see an unabashed and perhaps uncritical admiration, my found texts and assemblages were not exact copies, my intention had been to *participate* in the conversation, not to reproduce what had already been produced. At first I was hurt, embarrassed, ashamed, then I went to the library, looked at *The History of Art* by H.W. Janson and realized that in the art world there are no new, fresh images. Everything is a palimpsest, and behind that, another palimpsest. Even so, these rumors and words wormed into people's brains and poisoned my reputation, right as the artistic group began to gain national attention in Chicago and Minneapolis; I no longer received invitations to basement bowling alleys or damp attics or absurdist theater performances or group shows or Biennales, over the course of a summer I was expelled from the artistic group, I was driven out like a leper. I wanted to shake people's shoulders and scream, everything in the world is a palimpsest, motherfuckers! But no one would meet with me; no one returned my calls. I retreated to my hovel, a disgusting basement apartment in a decrepit part of town not even multi-billionaire international investors were able to rescue. I stopped getting dressed or going anywhere, which was a convenient time to do that, since my adult acne had flared up. *Life was taking revenge on me*. For a month or so, I sat in a basement 2
room with dim light and hatched a plan to escape. In the end I had transformed my mildly beautiful self into a functioning hermit with a sour taste in her mouth. I no longer carried myself with an artistic aura. I started to hunch over if I went anywhere,

which was seldom. I used to be a relational person, I thought, until people decided they wanted nothing to do with me.

How is someone supposed to live like that?

I decided to start over. I moved to New York City, a city that no one from Milwaukee imagined moving to a) because no one who lived in Milwaukee ever dreamt of leaving in the first place and b) because the cost of living in New York City is expensive, astronomically so. But I lived cheaply there on quinoa and rice. Or perhaps the word is frugally. I was sane in that astronomically expensive city living life frugally like an urban peasant. It took me years to find a stable living situation, yet I was saner than I had ever been in my entire adult life. Helen Moran, a sane and functioning adult in New York City: how? How is it possible to keep your sanity and exist on crumbs in the drawer?

You'll see, I said to no one. I'll show you. Someone will pay me one day to divulge how I lived so frugally, elegantly, and sanely in that glittering, amorally rich, and enormous hellhole.

4

AS I WOKE UP FROM A DREAM, the stewardesses collected trash. In my dream I was two women instead of one. We had been awarded a grant from a top-tier research-driven university to write a report on turtles nearing extinction on a remote and uninhabited island. Turtles: peaceful, monumental, stone-like creatures. When not dutifully writing our report, we were to be in charge of their feedings. We fed the turtles large, leafy plants the size of old gray desktop computers from the '90s. It was fun having a friend; we wore thick rubber gloves fitted over our hands that made it impossible to type out our report. A turtle bit us through the gloves and it felt like getting your fingers snapped in a mousetrap. The dream became a nightmare when we found ourselves in a morgue, standing before my adoptive brother's dead body spread out on an examination table, about to watch a man perform an autopsy as he rolled on his rubber gloves. We started crying, then one of us walked away, and I was alone again.

When I woke up, I noticed some of the stewardesses were wearing latex gloves, lightly powdered, and the powder traces could be seen dusted faintly across their shoulders and shirt-sleeves. If someone studied the traces, if someone put the traces under a microscope, perhaps they would detect a pattern that would unlock the secrets of the universe. I stretched my legs out as far as possible, then began to shift my attention to the purpose of my trip. To find out what happened to him, I said to no one, in other words, to investigate his suicide, to investigate the loss of a will to live. Demystify the pattern, and demystify the death. *His*
3 *death, his death, a death that I abhor*. I felt weeping in my eyes. I sniffled. The man sitting next to me asked if I needed a tissue.

I'm not crying, I said as I accepted it and dabbed my eyes gently.

It's just allergies, I said. Don't worry.

He had already turned his attention away to the in-flight magazine. As I sat there with my weeping, I thought it might be a mistake to expect to come away with an understanding of what happened. It might be a trap. I prepared myself to be satisfied with uncertainty even though I hated things that were uncertain or ambiguous. I disliked clouds, fog, certain types of philosophy, little children, and poetry. I preferred the concrete, the absolute, fiction and nonfiction. Because life is not poetry; life resembles fiction, life resembles the writing of the Greek tragedians, those foundational thinkers!

You're not flexible enough, my adoptive father once told me. Life is going to be very difficult for you, Helen, unless you learn to adapt to changes. Be flexible. Be a better person. Be a better daughter.

The stewardess gestured at me. Ma'am, seats in upright position.

Everyone always called me ma'am for some reason.

I'm thirty-two, I said under my breath as I stuffed the soiled tissue into the seatback pocket.

Then I remembered that I packed my headphones, the noise-canceling type. I took them out; I liked to use them as earplugs, even at my shared studio apartment, I wore them on nights when my roommate Julie had her boyfriend over, so I wouldn't be forced to listen to their disgusting, noisy genitals smacking against each other. Someone gave them to me as a gift, or perhaps someone loaned them to me and forgot to ask for them back.

I stared out at the gray and brown flat grids laid out simply and locked together like pieces of a child's puzzle, then I looked down at the lake, glass-smooth like a French bistro tabletop. I pictured my adoptive parents' house, and for a moment, I pictured the black sweater's arrival in a cardboard box, addressed to Helen Moran. It was with great pleasure that I pictured myself trying on the sweater, a perfect fit. Then I remembered I was going to my childhood home for a horrific reason. My eyes continued to water until the plane landed, and I took a taxi home.

I have always preferred not to pay too much attention to interstitial spaces like the space between landing and arriving, bland, forgettable spaces without texture, oatmeal spaces. I knew the ride home would take twenty minutes. During that interstitial space, the sky became darker and darker as if someone were slowly placing a black blanket over my eyes. My stomach trembled, saliva welled up inside my mouth, I swallowed it, I tried to trick myself into thinking I had just sipped a refreshing glass of spring water. A teacher said to do that. Instead of letting us go get a drink of water, she told us to think of a Swiss mountain stream and to swallow our saliva. The taxi crawled forward like a beetle through the suburbs, stopping and starting, stopping and starting, and I saw in my head the nunnery where all the nuns died and the priests took over, the pharmacy that housed a child-pornography ring, the bird sanctuary where a governmental agency collects the geese to feed to wolves.

It had been years since I had been to my childhood home to see my adoptive parents. It was by some unspoken agreement that as my adoptive parents and I became older we would come into contact less and less, although I couldn't say for certain why that was. I didn't even tell them I left Milwaukee until months after the fact. At the time it satisfied me to do that to them; to disappear for a while felt like getting some kind of revenge, because throughout the eighteen years I lived with them, they each on various occasions asked me to leave, to move out and find a new place to live. In the end, I suffered for my revenge, because when I moved to New York, unspeakable things happened to me.

Everything bad went around in a circle. Gray pocked streets and black skies filled my head like heavy stone tablets, causing me to feel a throbbing pulse near my left temple. In the pitch-black darkness, I felt the taxi coast down the hill of my childhood memories causing tears to come to my eyes, a physical descent that must have been buried deeply in my subconscious, and so we arrived at my adoptive parents' house, the house of Morans.

I don't want to be here any longer than you, and therefore I'm hoping my stay will be very brief, I said to the driver as

I gave him two wrinkled twenties, twenties I grabbed from my roommate Julie's desk.

I asked for change; when traveling it's always useful to have a little cash. The taxi left and I stood for a while outside the house. I put away my headphones. It began to rain. In silence I walked around the backyard, through the oak trees and bushes as a few motion-detector lights switched on and swept across my lone figure at a delay. By the time I made my way to the front door, my coat and shoes and canvas suitcase were soaking wet.

I rang the bell and the door opened. I was greeted by two little astonished ghost-figures clinging to each other for dear life. Helen, my adoptive parents said, we weren't expecting you! They were taken aback. No, it wasn't entirely clear to anyone, not even to the two who had raised me, how I had ended up at the front doorstep of my childhood home in soaking wet clothes. They appeared to be shocked by my canvas suitcase. Instead of greeting me pleasantly, they were whispering to each other.

5

HOW WAS IT THAT NO ONE was certain Sister Reliability would return home after her very own adoptive brother passed away? I might have been a monster, but not that kind of monster. It hurt me a little, that my adoptive parents were not expecting me, that they were so astonished by my arrival, that they seemed scandalized by my suitcase, by the mere suggestion that I would be staying a few nights with them in my childhood home. I supposed if they themselves had called me, I would have been able to tell them my travel arrangements. Instead a stranger called me, a relative I hadn't spoken with in years, a relative I saw last at a great-aunt's funeral I was forced to attend when I was in fifth grade. Uncle Geoff who once refused to own a phone! I don't think he was even my real uncle! He was probably a second cousin twice removed!! How avoidant they are! I thought. They couldn't bring themselves to tell their own adoptive daughter her adoptive brother was dead, the person she grew up with, the one she was forced to take baths with, tepid baths before he was toilet-trained, the one who pissed in the bath while she, the adoptive sister, sat calmly in a tub filled with a combination of tepid water and his urine, they didn't have the mental and emotional strength to tell her that he was gone, and not only was he gone, he did it to himself.

At first I wasn't upset that I had heard the news from Uncle Geoff, but now that my adoptive parents were standing right before me, I wanted to scream at them for subjecting me to such a senseless phone call from a stranger, the type of phone call that causes the brain to work so hard, the brain comes apart like pieces of dried-up clay and the next minute all one can see is a screen of flat, broken-down boxes, no more thought-secretions oozing out like toxic slime. My adoptive parents continued whispering to each other. Or maybe I heard the sound of the wind moving the tops of the trees around and the raindrops pelting the leaves and branches.

After all these years, she's just going to show up. Has Helen gone mad? I swore I heard them say.

No, it's the rain, I said gently, calmly. Haven't you two noticed we're in the midst of a terrible rainstorm?

Your mother and I can see that, said my adoptive father as they stood in the door frame.

They continued to stand in the door frame as the wind blew the rain through the open door. I made a note to myself that they had not greeted me with a plate of cookies and milk, not even tea and stale muffins, as I had pictured. Then I forced my way into the house because I was certain my adoptive parents were too astonished by my sudden appearance to invite me in.

Where do you keep the mop? I said.

My adoptive parents' mouths opened even wider and I saw the ugly fillings in their teeth, mostly silver and a few gold caps and some white sealants.

The mop, I demanded. And a bucket. Can't you see the floor is soaking wet? You have almost an inch of standing water here.

My adoptive mother pointed with a trembling finger in the direction of the utility closet down the hall next to the laundry room, and I went about making myself useful, mopping up the rain with broad, sweeping gestures and then wringing out the rain with all of my brute strength.

I could kill a dog with a brick! I shouted to no one when I was done.

After I finished mopping up the rain that had pooled in the foyer of my childhood home, after I went upstairs and threw open all of my bedroom windows to air out the stench of death, after I looked around my simple childhood bedroom, the most elegant room in the house because of its simplicity and lack of decorative knickknacks, after I emptied the contents of my canvas suitcase onto the carpeted floor, and changed out of my soaking-wet clothes into a gray, worn-at-the-elbows terrycloth bathrobe without a belt, I made my way downstairs where I knew my adoptive parents were waiting for me.

6

I FELT A SENSE OF VERTIGO as I went down the staircase, like I was traveling into an abyss.

Once I reached the living room, my equilibrium was only slightly restored. The room was brightly lit, overcompensating for the dark-wood-beamed ceiling and the dark orange wallpaper. No one liked the dark orange wallpaper, but they were too cheap to fix it. It was like looking at a movie screen with a flickering hair. After a moment, my eyes adjusted.

My adoptive parents motioned for me to sit down on a three-person-length wicker-basket couch in the living room, ostensibly to discuss the odd circumstances surrounding the death of my adoptive brother. My adoptive father sat on the couch with me, and my adoptive mother sat in a wicker-basket chair opposite the couch.

Where did all of this wicker furniture come from? I said to them as I looked around.

It was on sale, said my adoptive mother. It's easier to keep clean than the leather.

But besides that, not much has changed, said my adoptive father. You see Helen, all we did was replace the leather with the wicker.

The furniture was exactly the same, just of a different material and texture. The same family photographs and knickknacks graced the fireplace mantel, the stereo and speakers were set back in a black cabinet with a clear plastic door that, when pressed, swung open, and in the corner of the room was a smug and self-satisfied beanbag chair that the long-dead family dog used to sleep upon. I was shocked my adoptive parents had kept that beanbag chair all those years.

Who sits on that? I said to my adoptive parents.

That was Bailey's bed, said my adoptive mother, and she had a faraway, dreamy look in her eyes.

As soon as we clarified the matter of the new furniture, my adoptive mother, in her to-the-floor flannel nightgown, got up. Does anyone want some herbal tea? she said. I'm going to make some herbal tea.

She went into the kitchen and busied herself for a while and I heard her opening and closing the wood cabinets absentmindedly.

It's the three of us now, said my adoptive father.

He perched himself on the edge of a couch.

So how long do you think you'll be staying with us, Helen?

Once a rather handsome man, he had taken on a shrunken appearance since the last time I saw him, and his brown hair had gone gray on top and white on the sides. The color of his hair changed because of the grieving and the loss, I speculated. What a toll it has already taken upon him and his physical appearance! It saddened me to see such a drastic physical transformation, *and so soon after the death.*

To answer your question, I said, I purchased a one-way plane ticket. I'm here to look into the abyss and to offer my support in whatever form it takes.

He nodded. His eyes were small and sad and brave like those of an endangered bird flying through a forest at dusk. It has something to do with the death, I thought as my gaze shifted from my adoptive father to the beanbag chair to my adoptive father's hair, from his hair to the photographs on the mantel and from the photographs back to my adoptive father.

What a difficult time, I whispered as I scrutinized his appearance for a few more minutes, what a toll all this has taken, then I began to look at my adoptive father with the charity of a nun as I felt something foreign swell in my heart for him and his shrunken, birdlike figure. I moved closer to him on the couch, close enough to see the long white hairs growing behind his ears. Someone should trim those, I said.

What's that?

I wanted to offer him as much support as possible.

Your hair looks different, I said.

We haven't seen each other in five years, he said. People get older, Helen, people change. Besides, that's not what we're here to talk about. Do you have a job you have to return to? How long exactly will you be here? We will be hosting some visitors…

What visitors?

I was very curious, then I looked again at the beanbag chair slumped over in the corner of the living room and I let out a laugh. My adoptive mother came out from the kitchen to see what was wrong.

What a toll it has taken, this death and grieving and loss! I said under my breath, under my laughter.

My adoptive father said something to my adoptive mother.

Helen, said my adoptive mother, and she touched my shoulder. Is now not a good time to talk about what happened? Is being here at home with the two of us upsetting you?

4 My laughter, *now hardly weltering, died away*. I shook my head no.

It's fine, I said.

What was the concept of time anyway, especially to these two ghost-figures and their grieving? A few moments passed in silence and I wondered how many phantoms were in the living room with us that night. It was an appropriate question because as I was sitting on the three-person wicker couch, I started to formulate a hypothesis that their grieving was the fourth, yet-unspoken presence in the living room and no one had acknowledged it.

Perhaps I was the only one, the chosen one, who could see it clearly in a material way. If it had to take on a bodily form, and if I had to describe that form to someone, I would say I imagined it looked like a European man in his forties, average build and height, balding, with a red nose, sitting on a chair, observing us from a dark corner of the room, opposite the beanbag chair. I shook my adoptive mother's hand off my shoulder, got up from the wicker-basket couch, and reached out my own hand to touch their grieving and it recoiled *as if I were some sort of vagrant beggar*.

I am not a vagrant beggar! I shouted at it.

The European man who seemed to embody their grieving got up from his chair and left haughtily.

Perhaps this isn't a good time to discuss things, said my adoptive mother. You see, your father and I have been thinking... We can't be much of a support to you in a time like this, you see... do you understand what I'm saying... we can't support you right now, as it is, we're both trying to adjust to the situation...

Her voice trailed off and she floated back into the kitchen.

My adoptive father looked uncomfortable; I thought it might be a kind gesture to change the subject.

Will you vote yes in the stadium referendum? I said. My adoptive father covered his face with his hands.

It's worse than a car accident, I heard him say into his hands, it's worse than a house on fire.

My adoptive mother came out from the kitchen and set down a tray of chamomile tea and biscotti.

Helen, try to be nice to your father. Let's be kind to one another, after all, this is a difficult time for all of us, she said.

What a difficult time! I acknowledged again and again. What a toll it has taken! It had been less than 48 hours after his suicide. What would the weeks, the months, the years do to them, these ghost-figure survivors? I estimated they would live for another twenty to thirty years, meaning two to three more decades of post-traumatic living. Meanwhile, my adoptive mother and adoptive father sat on the wicker furniture and ate their crackers nervously. I attempted to explain that I was partially employed as a supervisor of troubled young people at an after-school facility designed to keep them off drugs, out of gangs, etc.

So you look after people? said my adoptive mother. You take care of them?

She looked at me incredulously.

Of course, I said, they are troubled.

Then I went into explicit detail about what my troubled young people encountered and endured. I told them in the quietest voice possible about the drug-addicted family members, the daily abuse meted out by once-trusted relatives, teachers, and coaches, the rapes and tortures. My adoptive parents shuddered.

I stared in disbelief at the beanbag chair. Dirty beanbag chair, shabby polyurethane-filled piece of shit! Their entire lives, they each had trouble hearing difficult and upsetting things; it astonished me that they were even able to accept the fact that their adoptive son committed suicide. I continued to stare at the disgusting beanbag chair. Over a decade ago, when the family cat died, they refused to remove the dead body. Everyone loved the cat, because it acted like the dog. They left the dead cat in the foyer, where anyone who entered the house encountered it. After two weeks of the dead cat on the floor, I became so disgusted with the sight and smell, I had no choice but to call pest-control services, the same service that scraped the dead animal out of my adoptive brother's closet. After they removed the rotten cat-body, everyone, including my adoptive brother, became very angry with me, and refused to talk to me for two months.

Do you remember Chad Lambo, Helen? Does the name ring a bell? He's been supporting us like we're part of his own family. He says he went to school with you, that you might know him.

What Chad? I said. I don't remember a Chad.

You don't remember Chad Lambo?

I don't know a Chad, I said, and I don't care to.

My adoptive father gulped down his tea, got up from the couch and went to the cabinet above the stereo and took out a bottle of gin, which he proceeded to pour into his empty teacup.

So it's just the three of us, I said, echoing my adoptive father.

They each frowned. I thought they were displeased, but it could have been about anything; there was nothing good in the situation. My adoptive father looked particularly angry. I thought he was going to ask me to leave the house again.

Helen, he said, I think it's time to go to sleep.

Had it really been five years since we had seen each other? Or was my adoptive father becoming senile?

I'll put fresh sheets on your bed, said my adoptive mother, and she stood up.

Tears the temperature of near-boiling water sprang out of my eyes for no reason, no reason at all. It was humiliating to cry in front of them as an adult. Ashamed, I ran up the stairs.

7

THE FIRST NIGHT BACK in my childhood bedroom, after a five-year-long absence, I sat on the carpeted floor and arranged my clothes and items into neat piles, I distracted myself from the miserable circumstances that brought me back to the fortress. To put my clothes and things into order was better than meditation, I thought, and much more productive. Arrange your room and you can arrange the world, I said to no one. Once I was finished organizing my things on the floor, I made my way into the closet, a walk-in filled with objects in chaos: a poster of silver dolphins swimming peacefully in a neon-green radioactive ocean, several books about crime including the O.J. Simpson trial, JonBenét Ramsey, Jeffrey Dahmer, one acid Western paperback, a photo of ten nude men on a ten-seated bicycle, aviator sunglasses, a fisherman's hat with the initials BC, a high school yearbook, two Fiona Apple CDs, a poster of Fiona Apple in her underwear crawling out of a couch, a worn Dover edition of *The Odyssey*, with many lines enthusiastically highlighted in the first few chapters. I set it down and paged through the yearbook until I realized it wasn't my yearbook, because I couldn't find a picture of myself; it was my adoptive brother's, 2003, a couple years after I graduated. I examined the well-meaning end-of-school-year messages from a few friends, I counted five signatures, inscribed with black markers and pens on the inner cover. I remembered one of the friends, Zachary Moon. He wrote: HAVE A GOOD SUMMER YOU FAGGOT. Smiley face. There were crude little drawings of bongs and breasts and vaginas and cars. YOURE MOMS CUNT. YOURE SISTERS TWAT. As I paged through the senior portraits, I became enchanted by all of the mocking and bitter faces. Everyone was broken and ruinous.

I crawled into bed, exhausted from my arranging, and immediately I felt the flower-patterned comforter from my childhood smother my adult female body. It made the skin under my breasts sweat, and the sweat soaked through my nightshirt, a gigantic men's XXL Hanes V-neck I found wadded into a soiled ball on an empty seat in the F train on St. Patrick's Day. I took off my shirt and threw it onto one of the piles on the floor. My breasts were the size of small, shrunken apples. The horse-pulling-the-cart image came into my mind as I wiped the sweat onto the comforter, and instead of the smell of apples, the smell of cucumbers wafted into the air, causing me to gag. I expected to find peace in my childhood bedroom, but not even opening the windows to let the room air out for hour after hour would release the stench of death and cucumbers permeating the room, and the house, a house of death.

8

ONCE UPON A TIME the house was infested with silverfish. They came out of the cupboards and closets in great numbers, they came out of every single crevice of the house, from the cracks in the ceilings to underneath the doors. Some men in hazardous-material outfits drizzled pesticide over the entire house, a pesticide which left a chemical residue that we were forced to inhale for weeks upon weeks because my adoptive father was too cheap to put us up in a hotel while the poison tapered off. Sometimes I thought we might have become brain-damaged from the fumes, each of us sustaining catastrophic brain injuries, it would have explained so much.

9

MY FACE BEGAN TO ITCH as I thought of the pesticide. Small hives pimpled up and down my cheeks and clustered at the sides of my nose. To calm myself, I thought of a waterfall, *a coping strategy* I learned from a coworker who experienced post-traumatic stress syndrome after she saw a person get hit by a truck in Tribeca.

The body exploded into pieces, she said, and the pieces flew all over, and some of it sprayed me in the face. How am I supposed to live with that? Whenever I think about the situation, and I can't help but think about it, every day, and at night before

I fall asleep, if I sleep, I begin to feel the spray hitting my face, so my therapist told me to think of a waterfall, a beautiful, peaceful waterfall.

It was called The Waterfall Coping Strategy. An image flashed in my own mind of a waterfall, even though I had never seen a waterfall in person. I had seen a watermill, so I switched to that image, to make myself more comfortable: a broken-down watermill surrounded by a forest in autumn. My adoptive mother brought us there when we were young, at a time when her hobby was photography. She took black-and-white photos of familiar objects close up, on a micro level, transforming everyday objects into something unrecognizable and monstrous. I hated those photos; I thought they were disgusting, they made me think of pores on a face. As soon as the image of the watermill and her photography phase settled comfortably into my brain, I saw my adoptive mother taking pictures of the oak leaves in various stages of decay. She zoomed in on the pattern of holes that punctured a leaf's tenuous fabric, while my adoptive brother and I hid behind the watermill. He was nine years old and I about to turn twelve, a repulsive time for me as I was just beginning to menstruate. Together, he and I had invented a game, because our adoptive parents were far too cheap to buy us board games or video games.

You each have the faculties to create your own games for fun, they told us. All you need is your imagination.

We made up a game called CONFESSION.

Do you ask for forgiveness of your sins? I said to him.

I played the priest, naturally, because I was older and more mature.

I want to confess my sins, Father. He bowed his head.

Go ahead, young man.

Last week I lied to our parents. I told them I had after-school baseball practice, but I didn't. It's not even the season for baseball, and besides, I'm terrible at it.

What did you do instead?

I went to the park with Max and we brought a magnifying glass. The sun was out, shining brightly, and there was a little boy there by himself. We snuck up behind him, grabbed his arms, and held him down against the gravel, Max rolled up the little boy's shirt, and I burned his back with the glass. He had pale skin. Max and I watched the sunlight laser into it and burn him. I remember he had freckles and moles. We burned his skin with the sun. Before we let him go, I realized he was much younger than I thought, probably four or five years old. I think he wet himself, because he smelled like urine. And for this, Father, I ask for forgiveness.

Do you understand that lying is one of the gravest sins, I said, worse than stealing, worse than kidnapping?

I told him he would have to humiliate his body in some way, in order to atone for his sins and the harm he did to the little boy. He threw himself into a pile of leaves and rolled around, and he suddenly looked old, in the sun-dappled dark, and at that moment it occurred to me that one day we would both be dead, composting like leaves and garbage in the worm-ridden earth. After a few minutes of rolling around in the leaves, he sat up and asked if he was forgiven.

You're going to die at some point, I said, and it's over. It's really over. It doesn't matter if you're forgiven or not. It's made up, it's all pretend. Do you understand? It doesn't matter!

I saw my adoptive mother come up from out of nowhere like a shadow and she began to wipe his face with a brown greasy napkin from a fast-food restaurant.

Why do you have dirt all over your face? she said. What kinds of filthy things have you two been doing?

When she was done wiping my adoptive brother's face, she strode right up to me and struck me across the face.

No adoptive mother of mine! I cried as a red star spread its points across my cheek.

That morning, she had leaned over eleven-year-old-me to shove the tampon up my vagina, because I was unable to do it on my own, it was always a trial to get the tampon up and into my vagina without the feeling of something being torn. She and my adoptive brother were the people closest to me in life, based on the sheer amount of time we once spent together. That afternoon with them, I skulked in the shadows and ate a heel of stale crusty bread meant for feeding the ducks. I was full of competition; I have always experienced extreme fits of jealousy, the type of jealousy that destroys the peace.

10

HELEN, WHY ARE YOU SO UNHAPPY? my adoptive mother would ask me over and over throughout the years of my childhood and adulthood. Why do you hate yourself so much? she would ask. It wasn't true! I argued as a child and adult. I was very happy and always had been. It was true to this day; I even found happiness in the free bagels my organization sometimes provided during work meetings! Would an unhappy and miserable person find perfect peace and contentment in stale bagels with no cream cheese?

It irritated me to be irritated in relation to my adoptive parents.

Your mistake is to isolate yourselves from us, she once said to me, you have an entire system of support at your disposal and you don't use it.

And not only that, you refuse to use it, my adoptive father said. It's hurtful to all of us.

I thought it was only a little funny that my adoptive brother seemed to have the final word on their system of support. Underneath my laughing, I was sobbing, and then my sobbing turned quickly into anger. They didn't even offer me cookies and milk, they were so astonished by my arrival. They didn't think I would come, I, the most reliable one of them all! There are so many people in the world, I thought, what do they do with themselves everyday? How to live, what to do? Hey Sister Reliability, suck my dick! If you wanted to show your gratitude, you could bake a pie tomorrow, wake up, find a recipe online, make a list of ingredients, go to the grocery store, pay for everything out of your own pocket, bake an apple or cherry pie, even though you have never baked a pie in your life. You never would. Be a better daughter, Helen. I heard my adoptive father's voice over and over in my head. Where's your fucking waterfall? I said to no one. You're not that type of person, a pie-baker, and you never were! My waterfall is a watermill in ruins!

I would need to begin first thing in the morning. I would shower off the dirt and death molecules I had accumulated since entering the house of my childhood, I would burnish my skin clean until *my thoughts began to burnish, sprout, and swell*, I would
5 dissociate myself from the death stench permeating the house. Hey Sister Reliability, kiss my cunt!

Instead of baking a pie, I search on the internet for old friends of his if he had any, teachers, doctors, therapists, dentists, etc., then scour his bedroom and disgusting closet for clues, I go out the window to examine the roof over his head, to cap off the day I sit down at the kitchen table with my adoptive parents, I could see already the bright overhead light illuminating their grief-stricken ghost-faces, I ask them pointed questions about his mental state the day of his suicide, what did he look like that day, what was he wearing? I interrogate them. Certainly something good would come from that, which would counter the terrible circumstances that produced his suicide.

What were your last words to my adoptive brother? What did you say to him before he went headfirst into the abyss?

THE FIRST REAL DAY

11

OCTOBER 2ND, THE FIRST REAL DAY of my investigation, it was pitch-black outside, darker than the darkest mornings in Manhattan when the garbage has not yet been collected and the rats are at work. That morning I was only able to wake up because I heard voices from below, loud and emphatic voices joking and laughing, disrupting my peace! I waited until the voices subsided and when I went downstairs to investigate, I was astonished to see a man I had never seen before sitting at the table, wearing a gray suit, reading the newspaper, and sipping coffee as if he had been a lifelong resident or an esteemed guest of my childhood home. All the kindness and generosity I worked so hard to muster up that morning dissipated quickly.

Who are you? I said. What are you doing here?

The man looked at me and removed his round rimless glasses.

I'm Chad, the grief counselor, the man said, you must be Helen.

Helen Moran, I said.

I didn't extend my hand, because it didn't seem like that kind of social meeting; it was like meeting an emergency relief services worker, I thought, and you don't shake those people's hands.

Chad stood up from the table and extended his hand as toast crumbs fell down the front of his suit.

I touched his hand lightly, the way I would touch a sick person. So how do you know them?

We go to the same church, he said.

He smiled.

Helen, do you remember me?

Without his glasses, he appeared to be around my age.

We went to school together, he said. We were in the same homeroom for sophomore year, Mrs. Kleeb. I sat across from you and your friend.

I searched my memory thoroughly for Chad in high school, but no image came up. Not even one image to tamp down quickly.

You've altered your appearance, I said.

Well, I'm older now, he said.

As are you, he said a little less generously.

It horrified me to think a stranger who knew me from sixteen years ago was now sitting in my childhood home, eating his breakfast, and talking to my adoptive parents about the suicide, maybe even consoling them with religion, and offering his own version of support. He probably knows more than I do about the situation, I thought with disgust.

I have been very interested in seeing you again, he said. Your parents have told me a lot about you.

That time of my life was terrible. It was a depressing time. I've lost weight since then. Of course my skin is worse than in high school.

I don't notice it, he said. And your parents do have a lovely house here.

Appalled, I put a piece of bread in the toaster, then I began to empty the dishwasher and I heard him speaking to me. It was just a voice in the background. Meanwhile, it was very pleasant to take things out of the dishwasher and to put them in their correct places, the places I remembered from childhood chores, chores to get one extra dollar a week. My cheapness began in early childhood, because my allowance was so small, it was incredibly disheartening to try to save up for something big, like a bike or a video-game system. It was easier to make do without. Then I noticed Chad was smiling at me and speaking and occasionally gesturing with his hands. I started to actually listen when I detected a bitter note in his voice.

It's terribly difficult to be a family friend and a therapist. What are you up to these days?

At least he didn't call me ma'am, I thought. I told him I helped troubled youth and for emphasis, I slammed shut the dishwasher. He put on his rimless glasses and peered at me.

So we're not that different, he said. We can understand each other.

Contrary to his claim, it was very difficult to understand him that dark, damp morning. It was difficult to locate my attention and to direct it to him. My lack of focus, my isolation. Was that what the poets called solitude? When we become adults, we leave behind the solitude we once enjoyed as children. Perhaps I was overwhelmed by this person from my teenage years, someone who saw fourteen- or fifteen-year-old me, now sitting in my childhood kitchen under the worst possible circumstances. In fact, when he told me he was from my high school, and not just my high school, but from my homeroom, I thought I was hallucinating. He continued to say things, occasionally I discerned the phrases tumor in the mind and immense mental and emotional pain, and threshold of pain and will to live. The will to live! Was he talking about my adoptive brother? I wondered. I felt I had to say something.

But Chad, have you talked suicidal people down from the abyss?

He held up his hand at me like a traffic guard, continued speaking, and let his hand fall smoothly to his side. He was very pleased with himself and his mannerisms. He must have gone to Europe to learn that, I thought, he must have the conscience of a metal beam. Smooth and metal. A smooth, metal beam for the construction of a brand-new sleek and terrible building in a bad part of town.

I saw myself say excuse me and I stood up and wandered over to the kitchen sink and stared out the window above the sink but I was really looking at my own reflection because it was dark out, as if it were the middle of the night, and then right through the reflection of my face I saw a black street that snaked its way into a town where people spoke a dying language, population 666.

It was very simple, this black street that went through my face and through the window. It stretched on forever like an infinite snake. I made myself dizzy staring at my own reflection for too long, the reflection of my blotchy face, and my impossible, thick, coarse, and heavy hair that took up most of the window.

If you want to think of something sad, I said, think about all of the suicides people commit each day, hundreds of them do it, and consider the family members and husbands and wives forced into my position, the investigator! Behind every suicide, there's a door. If you open the door you might find out things you wish you never knew. Some people never open the door, they prefer not to know anything about the circumstances of the suicide, and they walk away and wash their hands clean.

No, I said. I will rip open the door immediately. I'm certain the door is made of paper. I will shred it into pieces, then step calmly through the frame.

Helen, I'm so glad you're talking with Chad, said my adoptive mother. Do you remember him from high school?

She approached me from behind in a white bathrobe. The reflection of the white bathrobe grew until it swallowed up the entire window. It looked like a ghost! She seemed pleased with herself for remembering the connection.

He has been extremely helpful to us, she whispered, he has been like a beacon of light.

I helped myself to a glass of refreshing water.

I don't remember him. What is he doing here?

I'm here to offer my support and guidance to you and your family, said Chad. I'm always available during a familial crisis.

No one told me this would happen, I said. I wasn't given any kind of warning!

Helen, did you get good sleep last night? interrupted my adoptive mother. You look a little tired.

It occurred to me that I had never been healthier, physically, in my life. Since coming to Milwaukee, a persistent and annoying day cough had gone away. My knees no longer ached from standing. My eyes were clear instead of fogged with mucous. The swelling of my ankles went down. My stomach settled. My hands stopped shaking. Pieces of earwax fell out.

I'm fine, I said. It just took me all night to unpack my suitcase.

My adoptive mother looked at me worriedly, while Chad smiled.

She says she's fine, he said, and she's probably right.

A few months ago I went to a free therapy clinic. It was free, I found out later, because they were conducting a study for a medical journal article. I only went because I wanted to know if there was a way to tamp down my anger, to stop disrupting the peace, my own included. You need a plan, said the therapist, who was actually a therapist-in-training. He prescribed a plan of thirty minutes of cardio a day, yoga twice a week, and one career aptitude test. I never went back.

Helen, said Chad, when was the last time you went to church?

I didn't say anything.

Don't be rude, said my adoptive mother. Helen, say something!

The reason we're gathered here like this, I said, is because someone killed himself.

My adoptive mother took out a tissue from her robe and began dabbing her eyes.

A lot of people kill themselves, I said, but it seems like most of them do it when they're older, like after they've reached middle age. We try everything we can to preserve ourselves and yet eventually something catches up with us, something dreadful creeps up, and we just can't do it anymore. Then we throw our lives away, into the trash heap of suicides.

Perhaps, said Chad, we would be more comfortable sitting in a different room.

The three of us moved into the living room. I seated myself in the wicker-basket chair opposite Chad and my adoptive mother on the wicker-basket couch. Someone had lit three white candles.

I was looking at Chad through the candlelight. Something about his sitting posture, too straight and upright, reminded me of someone. Suddenly, an image of a broad, muscular young man who wore sleeveless Champion t-shirts took root in my brain. Homeroom sophomore year was set up in a U shape, perfect for observing and critiquing. I sat across from a young man in a sleeveless shirt, and I would stare at his patches of shoulder acne, red and irritated. From far away he looked sunburned. He was a starting power forward on the basketball team, and, unlike a lot of his friends, he had a long-term girlfriend, a brunette girl, everyone thought they were the perfect couple until one day he got into a terrible car accident. He was in a coma for a weekend, phone calls were made, a prayer chain was activated, and when he woke up, he couldn't remember his girlfriend or how to dribble a basketball. It was one of the great tragedies of our high school. This person from my high school was named Chad Lambo. After the car accident, he became much friendlier. He even tried to befriend me in homeroom, which at the time I thought was disgusting. Presently Chad Lambo had invaded my childhood house and offered his support and guidance to my adoptive parents. *I was the one that was supposed to offer them my supportive beam of light*! Perhaps he would take the place of the adoptive son they once had, and lost. As soon as I thought that, I gagged with force.

It's the water I drank, I said apologetically to everyone.

No one cared. I heard my adoptive mother tell Chad Lambo a couple of stories about my adoptive brother; at the moment, they were too depressing for me to digest. He must have said something very moving in response because she began to cry. Suddenly, for no reason at all, I remembered that one of my favorite troubled young people once described his girlfriend as a short woman with a uterus that felt like a bundle of dried-up twigs.

It hurts my dick, he said to me when I had him over for dinner at my shared studio apartment.

A bundle of dried-up twigs! No uterus of mine, I said or I thought. I folded my hands in my lap pleasantly, because I had made a lifetime of studying elegant mannerisms. I folded my hands immaculately in my lap and said that I thought the religious apparatus was a bunch of dried-up twigs; I left out the part about the uterus hurting the dick.

No one heard me. Chad Lambo asked us if we knew why our family was special and unique. No one said anything. My adoptive mother cried and blew her nose into the tissue. He said something about the adoption of Moses, how he had been discovered in a basket hidden behind the reeds along the Nile during the time of the Egyptians and their slaves, then, changing the topic abruptly, he began a terrible story about undiscovered tumors of the mind. I thought it was tasteless, the way he was bringing religion and the Bible into the conversation. He didn't even get to the part about Moses and the burning bush. I might have heard him say *cancerous brain tumors*, how they can take root invisibly, bulbous tumors the size of grapes, how not even trained medical professionals are able to detect the invisible grapes, how people with these cancerous grapes go about their days like everyone else and no one can tell that the cancer is slowly eating up all the brain cells until one day, after the person kills himself, we can then, and only then, look upon the person after death and say, perhaps the grapes took root in his brain.

I stood up and went to the bookshelf and stared at the spines. There were encyclopedias, a whole shelf of obsolescence. There was one book in particular I kept staring at. It was as if someone were shining a spotlight on it. It appeared to be a book about cars. I took it off the shelf, a hardcover doorstopper with bright glossy photographs, and I began to flip through the pages, and Chad Lambo continued speaking about the location of my adoptive brother's soul, about the possibility of a soul being in extreme distress shortly after dying in a violent manner, as if he were a priest, and the cars on the pages flipped past my eyes so quickly, it was like one multicolored, shimmering, flashing psychedelic car. I felt like I was on drugs.

Whose book is this? I interrupted.

My adoptive mother took the tissue from her face.

It was your brother's.

Then her face retreated into the tissue.

The living room began to spin a little. It *was* your brother's, she had said. She employed the word *was* not because it was no longer a book, but because my adoptive brother no longer owned it, because it could be said my adoptive brother no longer possessed anything. I collapsed onto the wicker-basket chair.

Was not is, I said.

Was not is!

When a person dies, it is the end of a human life, I announced.

Then I said or I thought, What a difficult time it is! What a toll it has taken! My adoptive mother and Chad Lambo continued to look at me in amazement and disgust, a disgust reserved for cockroaches.

Insulted, I stood up from the wicker-basket chair, and remembered how my roommate Julie once described her previous apartment in Chinatown. A couple years ago, her brother, a home renovator, opened up her kitchen countertop for some kind of do-it-yourself weekend project only to discover her entire kitchen counter, approximately fifty-five cubic feet, had been filled to the brim with live cockroaches, enough to fill four black garbage bags full of hissing wings and shells that were tossed promptly to the curb, and how even after the bags were tossed to the curb and collected, my roommate Julie vomited for five days straight, because she pictured the cockroaches' legs locked together and their hard shells clicking against one another in one giant cockroach-ball-mass underneath the counter where she prepared all her favorite meals. She used to love to cook.

It's enough to sicken you to death, I said as I turned around to face Chad Lambo and my adoptive mother, that such disgusting things can take place beneath the sterile surface, all the while you go about your daily life, eating and talking and gossiping and sanitizing and wiping things down and shitting.

The most we can do, I said, is to organize ourselves. Organization is good for morale. Make your bed.

I looked at my adoptive mother. Don't you remember you used to say that to us back when we had all the time in the world? It's one of the few things you said that turned out to be true. Organization has always been good, if not necessary, for the human spirit, even for those humans of the lowest common denominator, even for the most impoverished of souls. That's why the homeless bums and beggars in Manhattan situated themselves on pieces of cardboard with their few cherished belongings surrounding them like a moat: organization.

I turned away from them both, disgusted at life as described by the sciences, disgusted at all biological life, trillions of cells and nuclei and mitochondria and membranes and bacteria multiplying and squirming and trembling and teeming invisibly underneath our noses.

We're too dumb to see it, we're too brainless to see how disgusting it is, I said.

Here's what we'll do, I heard Chad Lambo say to my adoptive mother, we'll pray for her. We'll just keep praying for her.

12

THEY DIDN'T TRY TO STOP ME from leaving the living room when I told them Sister Reliability had important work to attend to.

You call yourself Sister Reliability? said my adoptive mother.

They call me Sister Reliability, I said as I reminded her of my position as overseer of troubled young people.

Before I excused myself, I asked them where my adoptive father was.

He's at work, too, said my adoptive mother.

He went back to work? I said, appalled. Why isn't he here grieving with us?

We all work on grief in our own ways, said Chad Lambo.

Thank you, I said with elegance.

I took the book about cars with me. I went back up into my bedroom, like a bug scuttling back into its crevice, furious with my adoptive father for abandoning us during this traumatic and difficult time. I managed somehow to find a patch of light for myself in the darkness of my childhood bedroom by looking at the book of cars, pictures of brightly colored, expensive-looking plastic and metal vehicles of death. When I set the book down, I noticed there was a sticker on the cover, a red circle that said HALF-OFF and then it was crossed out with a black marker and it said 75% OFF. It must have been one of those remaindered books on the clearance table, I thought. The cheapest book on the table, I bet, the cheapest book in the store! Everything in this house is so cheap, I laughed, even the most expensive things become cheap by merely existing inside this very house! Every item in the house that wasn't a piece of furniture functioned as a knickknack or decorative bric-a-brac purchased in bulk quantities as cheaply as possible from places like Costco and Pier One Imports. Look behind one knickknack and see ten in a row, all waiting patiently for their turn to be displayed. Then it dawned on me: I had finally come up with a formula that made sense of everything.

An alert went off on my cellphone, a loud and brash alarm that sounded like a madman hammering on a piece of tin. CALL SUPERVISOR TO CHECK IN it said. I attempted to leave a message on my supervisor's voicemail, to let him know I had safely arrived in Milwaukee.

Dear Supervisor, I said, I've finally formulated a theory of the house. I can't wait to tell my troubled young people about it. Everything is extremely cheap here, even life itself! I laughed.

I called him three times, aborting each message because of my laughter.

Also in case you've forgotten, I've lost my only adoptive brother, I finally managed to say on my fourth attempt at a voicemail, HE KILLED HIMSELF and I need to find out HOW. Then I hung up. My laughter died and I felt a shock of despair race through me. Tone is difficult to control, I thought unhappily, we say things in our heads and we hear them and they sound right and when we speak them, they sound completely different to others. My voice has always been deep, almost like a man's, and my laughter has always been the laughter of a monster, I despaired, and it only became more monstrous in proportion to the seriousness and finality of my adoptive brother's death. They locked people up for laughing too much. Out of the corner of my eye, the book about cars sparkled and flashed, troubling me. Perhaps it had been a gift from my adoptive parents to my adoptive brother, perhaps it was given to him for his birthday. It made sense to me, it followed my theory of the house that my adoptive parents would buy the cheapest book on the clearance table, forget to take the sticker off, and then give the book to their adoptive son for his birthday. They purchased for him a book about a subject he didn't care about, the cheapest book on the table, and they gave it to him for his birthday; they never understood one thing about either of us!

I realized I had created an entirely fictional narrative in my mind about the book of cars and its origins. Perhaps my adoptive brother bought it himself, perhaps he developed an interest in cars before he killed himself.

Of course he never bought himself anything. He never drank anything but plain water. He lived on white chicken and white rice. He left once, and then he came back. Then he left permanently. His exit was traumatic for everyone who knew him. Was it traumatic for him? He took tennis lessons one summer, then quit. He was forced to take an acting class for a summer, then quit. He worked for a week at a video-rental store, then quit. He wore the same clothes every day, the same light blue polo shirt and dark pants, and he talked to the same small circle of people. He never expressed an interest in dating, marriage, or having children. He didn't make mistakes. He had no credit. He stole things, then returned them and asked for cash refunds. For exercise he walked the family dog, now dead, too. He walked the same route around the block, never into the forest, then up the hill to the pharmacy, along the train tracks to the church parking lot and back. Sometimes, if he was in a particularly good mood, he would tie the dog to a bench and go into the ice cream place, where he ordered vanilla ice cream. No one orders vanilla ice cream, except depressed people! He stayed the same his entire life. He never changed. If he were a character in a Russian novel, he was flat not round. He lived like a starving peasant. If he had indeed bought something for himself, it would have been precisely the cheapest thing on the table. Did he even have an interest in cars?

I retraced my thoughts. No one in our adoptive family cared about cars, except inexpensive ones, cars on sale, used cars. Everyone in my adoptive family had a passion for sales. What was this book about expensive, colorful cars doing in the house? According to my adoptive mother, it belonged to my adoptive brother, but she was unreliable as a source; she was consistently confusing things, names, places, and people. Since I had been at home she called me my adoptive brother's name a few times.

Yoo-hoo! I heard a voice call out. Helen!

It was muffled, but it sounded like, Helen, we're leaving! And what was I supposed to say to that?

I opened the door.

Wonderful, I yelled back, I'm very glad for you!

It dawned upon me that the book was a gift from a stranger, a friend, a lover. Did he have lovers? I wondered. Did he have sex? No, it wasn't possible that my adoptive brother, who lived in his childhood bedroom for most of his life, had ever had sex. He was short, chubby in a not-unappealing way, and very self-conscious. He must have been asexual.

The garage door opened and closed. I looked out my bedroom window: the security light beamed down upon my adoptive mother and Chad Lambo in his sedan and the wind poured some more rain down upon the house. I spent the morning sprawled out on my childhood bedroom floor as I attempted over and over to formulate a plan for my investigation, but all I did was speculate. All of this speculation will lead you to nothing, I thought. You might speculate yourself to death.

13

IT HAS ALWAYS BEEN A DARK HOUSE set at the bottom of a
small and quiet hill surrounded by tall trees as leafy as the month
of June. The tops of the trees bristled like brushes against the 6
sky, even in the middle of autumn. The house did not get good light, not during the day, not during the summer, and especially not in the afternoon. On rain-dark days the entire house had the ambience of a medieval cellar.

I noticed some houseplants had died since I arrived; there were two on one of my childhood bedroom's windowsills, and the plants were covered in patches of bright red dots. Upon closer inspection I noticed that the dots were moving, the dots were crawling all over the brown stalks and leaves. Disgusted, I made a note to myself to take care of the dots, to find an insecticide in the garage. I had the entire house to myself. I set the book about cars aside and went into the hallway. My adoptive brother's bedroom door was closed. There was a strip of yellow light underneath the door because someone (perhaps my adoptive brother?) had left the lights on.

Staring at the strip, I became frightened of the room. I hadn't expected to have such a visceral reaction to his door, only a few hours ago I thought I would rip it open. I surprised myself; I shuddered as I walked past, and went downstairs and into the living room and kitchen, where I looked around. I noted that some knickknacks from my memory were missing, and that they had been replaced with new knickknacks, but the overall arrangement of the house had stayed the same. Old knickknacks had not been removed without being replaced with fresh, new knickknacks. The wicker replaced the leather, I said to no one.

What I needed to do was gather clues like some kind of gigantic clue-collecting agent and then put them into an overarching single theory-idea and perhaps this would answer the question of what led my adoptive brother to take his own life. Was I crying? One might have asked me, but no one was there.

Then the household phone did not stop ringing. After being startled out of my thoughts, I began to enjoy the ringing as background music. When the answering machine clicked on, it was my adoptive brother's voice offering a tentative, slightly garbled outgoing message.

This is the Morans, he said, we're not here right now, so please leave a message.

His voice, separated from his now-dead body, echoed through the kitchen and it chilled me to the bone!

We're not here right now, I said to no one, then immediately I began to sweat and I went into the living room and collapsed pitifully onto the wicker-basket chair. I must have looked insignificant as I sat in a crumpled heap, attempting to compose myself with steady inhalations and exhalations. He always had trouble enunciating things properly, I despaired. I listened to the outgoing message over and over. A thousand times, I heard his voice and I came to the realization: he never spoke clearly. He spoke as if he had rocks inside his mouth. Did he eat rocks? I wondered. Did my adoptive parents feed him rocks? No, to put it more precisely, he was always a husk of a human being, almost embarrassed or ashamed to be living and breathing and eating like the rest of us. He must have really hated himself, I said to no one as I got up to disconnect the answering machine.

The next time the phone rings, I'll answer it myself, I decided. And of course the phone kept ringing. Whoever called asked for my adoptive parents and had no idea who I was until I reminded them that one of us was still alive.

Oh, Helen, oh, how are you doing? the caller would say. Are you okay?

Oh yes, I am fine. I'm more concerned about my adoptive parents, all of this loss has taken a serious and perhaps permanent toll on them, but at least I'm here to help out. Would you like to leave a message?

I spoke to the callers in an artificially composed voice, a voice I myself barely recognized. And like a dutiful secretary, I proceeded methodically to take down a series of messages on a notepad in the smallest handwriting possible. Call Laura. Call Dr. Stein. Call Thomas. Call the funeral director's office. Call the gravestone specialist. Call the auto insurance company. Call the hospital. Writing down the notes cramped my hand. I am not a secretary, I said to no one, I am a detective and I need clues or at the very least ideas about where to find clues! I told myself I needed to look more closely at *everything*. I walked around the empty house, upstairs and down, to-ing and fro-ing like some kind of harmless perambulator. I picked up knickknacks and set them down. I sifted my hands through bowls of potpourri, and not even that sickly sweet perfume-odor covered up the death-smell permeating each room. I opened doors and closed them. Unlike everyone in my adoptive family, I have always had a fondness for doors. Doors are very important, I thought, but why? Perhaps because they have something to do with childhood, because we rarely notice doors as adults. I continued walking around the house. I discovered squeaky drawers inside kitchen and bathroom cabinets, and I adjusted them with a special tool, some kind of tiny screwdriver, so they would open and shut softly. Be a better daughter, I said to no one.

I enjoyed hearing my footsteps pad across the carpet. My shared studio apartment in Manhattan had wooden floors, always the squeaky wooden floors, never the soft padding of Midwestern carpets. In Manhattan I squeaked, in Milwaukee I padded. Then I began to feel as if the embodiment of my adoptive parents' grieving, the balding European man, were walking around the house with me, pointing out things that had escaped my observation, reminding me that it was my duty to investigate the house, to find some kind of answer, some kind of conclusion that would give me peace.

Maybe the answer is here, in this desk, he said, and he pulled open my adoptive mother's desk drawer where she kept her receipts and did her monthly budget.

There is nothing in here but receipts, I said.

Exactly, said the European man. He presented to me an inconspicuous envelope and an insurance bill with the name of a doctor and a phone number for the hospital.

This doesn't make any sense, I said. What does this mean?

The envelope was addressed to my adoptive brother.

I'm not the ghost, said the European man.

Of course you're a ghost, I said. But he had already disappeared. It wasn't fair to me how ghosts came and went as they liked, I thought as I stood alone in the kitchen. Were people who believed in the possibility of ghosts themselves ghosts? No one was around or I would have asked someone. No one was there to say.

14

OF ALL THE PHONE MESSAGES I took down that afternoon, one message stood out to me, shining brightly and teasing me like a jewel-clue in the rough. It was a message from a young man named Thomas and he wanted to speak to my adoptive parents as soon as possible. He sounded frantic, there was a real sense of urgency in his voice, a sense of urgency I had not heard since I landed in Milwaukee. The urgency in his voice occupied my thoughts until I saw myself go upstairs to get my phone.

Why did he sound so upset? I kept asking no one. Why does he sound like he's going to have a breakdown?

With swift, purposeful movements, I picked up my phone and dialed the number I had taken down.

The phone rang and rang and in between the rings I heard an electric silence like a refrigerator's steady and persistent hum, then the ringing and humming went away abruptly, and a voice said, Hello?

I was shaking uncontrollably. Speak! I screamed to myself, speak! My tongue felt like an inchworm inside my mouth and I became estranged from it.

Speak! I said and this time it was aloud.

The voice on the phone said, Yes, hello? Who is this?

I heard my voice trembling like a drop of water on a leaf when I said, Is this Thomas?

This is Thomas, said the voice, who is this?

It's his adoptive sister, I said, my name is Helen. I spoke to you when you called earlier.

I wanted to talk to your parents, he said.

I just don't understand, he said. His voice broke off.

I don't know if he ever mentioned he had an adoptive sister, I said gently, but here I am, you can tell me anything.

I know who you are. He's gone and you're the one that's left.

Yes, I know, do you know what happened to him?

Silence.

Who are you in relation to him?

I'm a friend, said Thomas, I was his friend. Can I call you later? Now isn't a good time to talk.

Of course. Leave a message if I'm not here.

He hung up before I was able to ask him if he had known anything about my adoptive brother's struggles, because surely my adoptive brother had struggled, had Thomas known he was suffering? I wanted to ask Thomas if my adoptive brother had mentioned anything about a plan, *a suicide plan*. We hung up without making an arrangement to speak later. Thomas, who was this Thomas? I wondered. A long time ago I went home one weekend expecting to see my adoptive brother, expecting to have long conversations deep into the night with him, only to discover he had gone on a road trip with a friend. The idea of him doing something as pedestrian as going on a road trip had shocked me. Did they go to Mexico? Las Vegas? Was the friend Thomas? From where did he know this person?

My adoptive brother never had many friends, my poor little hermit. He had always preferred solitude to company. He isolated himself in his childhood bedroom even as an adult, whereas I left Milwaukee immediately. He must have devoted himself to something, everyone needs a cause; I didn't know what it was yet, but I would find out, I assured myself. His trouble had always been attracting friends, whereas I had no trouble attracting them, my main trouble was keeping them. Our adoptive mother worried about it. Why don't you each bring a friend home for dinner? she would ask us. Why don't you invite friends over after school? The truth was neither of us cared to bring anyone into our adoptive parents' house, the cheapest house on the block, cellar-dark. Bring them over for dinner? Bring them over for white chicken and rice and milk? When I was in seventh grade I once brought over a friend, whom I had attracted by giving some of my lunch money, and the next day this greedy little once-friend went on to give a report to everyone at the lunch table.

Helen's Chinese and her brother's Chinese, but they're not all Chinese, she said laughing, the parents are white!

Everyone at the table laughed.

I'm Korean, I said to the once-friend, and you're a stupid white cunt! I put my sandwich under her chin, as if I were threatening her with a knife.

Little white bitch, I whispered, do you know what a cunt is? Do you have a definition?

A nun stormed over to intervene, grabbed my forearm, and began to drag me to the principal's office. The principal was a smaller, meaner nun. My adoptive brother watched the scene from his lunch table, sitting alone, picking at a piece of chicken with a plastic fork. I kept looking at him, but couldn't catch his eye.

He was as predictable as the plains! White rice and white chicken sustained him. No dark meat! Who else found an entire day's nourishment from a single glass of cold water? Who else paid money for a scoop of vanilla ice cream? It made sense to me that he stayed in Milwaukee even as a grown man, I thought, Milwaukee was the perfect place for a person like my adoptive brother. Not only a dreadful city like Milwaukee, but a dreadful house like my adoptive parents', and in the dreadful house, his childhood bedroom, the only place he was ever truly comfortable. He was comfortable anywhere he was not forced to confront his own physical discomfort with being alive. And any time he went away from Milwaukee, he always wanted to go back immediately. That pattern of going away and coming back began with sleepovers in childhood, in the middle of the night, he would wake up and leave the friend's house, frightening the people in the house, they would be left with no choice but to call my adoptive parents, and sometimes the police. Every time we took a family trip out of town, we had to assure him that everything in Milwaukee would be exactly the same when we came back. Look at all the houses, my adoptive father would say, and the people inside them. No one's going anywhere. It never worked;

his fears were limitless. And it only drew attention to the fact that he wanted to be back inside his own home. His entire life, he was afraid of the weather. Perhaps it was a cry of distress to be that plain and predictable. Of course I didn't hear it, I thought. I didn't hear anything.

15

MY EYES TRAVELED ACROSS the downstairs hallway near the back of the house. The hallway floor was wood, a dilapidated wood with deep crevices that collected dirt and dead skin cells. I had to wear shoes to walk its length or my soles would turn black. No one did a thing about it. Mice came out of the corners. The windows were filled with webs and carcasses. A vent whooshed on, spitting out dirty air particles. I didn't cough. I covered my face. I went and filled another bucket with water and bleach. I started to mop. The mop head turned black. Long strands of someone's hair and leaf-shaped clumps floated on the surface of the bleach water. For an hour or so I pushed the mop back and forth as helpfully as possible.

As I squeezed out the mop into the bucket, I remembered how I once helped him with his lines for the end-of-year show. He was ten years old, and decided out of the blue to participate. I was in the show already, every year another show, and when he announced it, I felt a palpable, creeping sense that he was going to steal my sunshine. A fucking vine crept up my legs and around my waist, and I thought at the dinner table in my twelve-year-old head: *He's going to steal my sunshine.*

I'm doing it just this one time, he announced at the dinner table. Then he promptly forbade our adoptive family to attend.

They can't come to see me? I said.

His role in the end-of-year show was a great surprise to everyone, because he didn't like unpredictable things, and there was nothing more unpredictable than the end-of-year show. It had never occurred to me that he himself was unpredictable at times, for example, his voluntary appearance in the end-of-year show.

For a week, I listened to him go over his lines for a watered-down version of Shakespeare for kids interspersed with joyful singing and dancing, by pressing my ear to his bedroom door each night after dinner. It sounded like someone speaking with marbles in their mouth. How will anyone hear him speak with marbles in his mouth? I wondered. How will anyone understand him? Finally, I decided to intervene. I knocked on his door, burst into his room before he answered, and began to go over the lines with him.

Enunciate! I shouted at him like an acting coach. Speak like a normal human! Watch your posture!

So it could be said that I helped him deliver a successful performance. I was once, and perhaps only once, a very helpful person to him. And that is my defense.

The day of the end-of-year show I came down with the flu and was forced to stay home. I wore my pajamas all day and was shut up in my bedroom like a leper. My adoptive mother watched him perform, because even though he had forbidden them to attend, she attended secretly. When it came to his life, she seemed to see her role as less a mother and more a detective.

He never tells us anything, she complained to me once. Does he tell you anything?

Absolutely not, I said.

Like a stalker, she snuck in when the lights went down and stood to the side of the front row in a dark area near the curtain. She took picture after picture of him, and as soon as the cast took a bow, she left so it would seem as if she had spent the entire night at home. I'll never forget how she came home beaming that night, beaming as if he had won a fucking Oscar. She broke the quarantine and came into my room.

Unbelievable, she said as she recounted her adventure. Who knew he could act like that? He's been hiding his talent from us all this time. He had them rolling in the aisles. He had the audience in the palm of his hand!

That night my adoptive brother never detected her presence; her plan was a success.

They gave him a standing ovation, she said. You wouldn't have believed it…

Because he gave such a wonderful performance that night, she registered him for acting lessons on the weekend. He was to attend SCENE ONE acting classes for kids, held in a plaza fifteen minutes away every Saturday morning that summer, where he would learn to sing, dance, smile, bow, etc. For once, my adoptive mother decided not to be cheap; I know for a fact one semester of classes cost over a thousand dollars. Of course he refused to go, but she forced him, and he was miserable the entire summer.

It was an unforeseen consequence of my assisting him, and I do not take any blame, I thought. Because of the nice thing I did for him, he had to do something he hated. It all equaled out. My adoptive father was against the acting classes, he hadn't witnessed the finesse of my adoptive brother's performance, he didn't understand why he had to write out a check for thousands of dollars to SCENE ONE, I overheard him say that he thought she imagined the whole thing. The only proof she attended the end-of-year show was a series of pictures she took. Years later, she told my adoptive brother that she had watched his performance from stage right; he didn't believe her, even though she never lied to us. He had a faraway look in his eyes, so she repeated herself.

I have pictures of you, she said.

There was no reaction. He acted as if she were talking about someone else, someone he knew in passing. By the time she told him she had attended, he had already detached himself from that experience. He was someone else and not familiar with the person in the end-of-year show. My adoptive mother always told us we were special, I thought, and the truth was we were both merely average. She never lied to us and she rarely said anything that turned out to be true.

Somewhere in this house there were photos of my adoptive brother performing in the end-of-year school play, the shining star of the night. I went into my adoptive father's wood-paneled study where I knew family albums were kept. I began to sift and sort through them. I picked up and examined a black-and-white photo of my adoptive father as a youth at a summer camp in upstate New York. He had a handkerchief tied around his neck, he was smiling. His family was as dysfunctional as they come! I said to no one. Each member was forced from early childhood to learn how to play or abuse Bach on the piano, violin, viola. He still occasionally abused the piano when he played Mozart or a little Schubert, no one else in my adoptive family liked Schubert, everyone else preferred when he played Mozart in the second living room, a formal room with a piano and leather chairs and nothing alive, the dog and cat weren't ever allowed in that room. When he played Mozart or Schubert the house filled up with white male European culture. We were expected to worship it, which we did for a while, but once I went to college, I stopped. There is a world and history of nonwhite culture, I wrote to them once in a furious letter. And you kept us in the dark our entire childhood! The two white people raised their Asian children to think Asian art was decorative: Oriental rugs and vases! Jade elephants! Enamel chopsticks!

Almost everyone on my adoptive father's side of the family, except my adoptive father, was burdened with some variation of a mental illness, usually a complicated one like schizophrenia, although the truth was I had endless patience for those with this particular mental situation, mostly because the majority of the troubled youth under my care and protection exhibited early signs of this terrifying and debilitating disease, I saw it in their eyes, I saw the schizophrenia in their pupils.

Sometimes I noticed when I took them off the facility grounds, their eyes scanned the streets of Manhattan as if some key to unlock the mysteries of the universe were to be discovered amidst the endless piles of garbage bags and garbage-people and it seemed to me nothing less than one of the first signs of schizophrenia, irrationality and madness at its finest, although of course I didn't think they needed to be locked up, as I was an active and vocal opponent of mass incarceration and the school-to-prison pipeline, I went to protests and rallies and enjoyed screaming angrily at people with others, but when I saw my troubled people staring distantly at the garbage piles, searching, searching, I concluded perhaps they should be locked up for the rest of their lives, then something would happen, one of the schizophrenic troubled people would do something nice, and I would reverse my position, I went back and forth over the matter and never came up with a definitive answer, either way, I waffled a great deal, but in the end anyone would say I tolerated their schizophrenia, I didn't really mind it.

The keys to the universe aren't in the garbage! I screamed at them in an attempt to jolt them out of their dangerous and delusional fantasies and then I offered them a thin glass pipe filled with potent marijuana.

I had always promoted early intervention at my workplace; I was a proponent of special medical intervention when it came to my troubled young people, intervention mostly through the administration of marijuana, which was illegal, but I felt it was my ethical duty to give it to them. It calms them down, as I had explained to my coworkers, it helps them focus on real things, they smoke it and they *mellow*.

My coworkers shut up about the matter as long as I provided them with their own personal bags of marijuana. Of course since it was as integral to the facility as the paper products for the toilets, I bought the drugs with the credit card used to purchase the paper products. Everyone who took care of the troubled young people loved marijuana; the functioning of the facility continued smoothly with this improvement made.

The most recent photo of my adoptive brother I came across was a picture of a birthday dinner, probably his last or the year before. It was from the time during which he attempted to grow a mustache. He was sitting at a restaurant table, a heavily frosted birthday cake in front of him, the candles flickering under his eyes. He was smiling stiffly for the camera. Was this before or after he received the discounted book about cars? His eyes looked so tired, he appeared to be exhausted by living, my poor dear hermit. The act was wearing thin! He wore a light blue polo, the same shirt he wore every day of his life, the shirt he probably wore even the day he committed suicide. It was possible. It was the style of shirt he wore to Catholic elementary school and beyond, thick and starchy, ordered in bulk quantities from a Lands' End catalog. I stared at his photo; he didn't even look that Korean, he looked Chinese, and every time we went to a Chinese restaurant, the waitress would ask if he was Chinese, but I would never be asked, because it was very obvious to everyone that I was Korean or possibly Tibetan. Growing up, we both admitted to one another that we wanted to be white. As little children we were told that if we prayed to Jesus Christ, if we spoke to Jesus Christ as if he were our friend, if we told him the deepest desires in our hearts, he would answer our prayers and grant us our wishes, as long as we believed in him with a pure abiding faith.

I want to be white, he said to me once.

I want to be white, too, I said to him.

Sometimes at night I pray to God that I will wake up and be white, he said.

I too have spent nights in prayer to our lord Jesus Christ that I would become white, I said.

We were nothing less than disappointed about being Asian and very ungrateful about being brought into this country, a country neither of us had asked to come into, and neither of us identified as Asian, we never checked the Asian box. If someone asked us our nationality, we usually said, *adopted*.

He was alone in the photo from his birthday. I imagined my adoptive parents sitting across from him at a restaurant. My adoptive mother would ask him to smile for a picture. I saw my adoptive brother order a bowl of plain rice, nothing added, no salt or butter or soy. After the meal, my adoptive father would pay the check but not without first inspecting each item on the check carefully, even requesting that the server bring back the menu to check the bill. Actually, now that I thought about it, a night like that would cause anyone to want to commit suicide!

Everything is fine, my adoptive brother wrote to me once, and then it isn't. Everything in my world is neutral, he wrote, and then it goes dark. Our house depressed me, childhood depressed me, school depressed me, our dog depressed me, my shoes depressed me, my books depressed me, you depressed me, our parents depressed me, the tree outside my window depressed me.

I knew then that his writing to me of everything that depressed him, in combination with his miserable birthday photo, was the first real clue that my adoptive brother had been thoroughly miserable before he killed himself. His suicide had not been *out of the blue*, it had been arranged and thought out. In order to find more photos of him as substantiating evidence, I had to flip past several grotesque photos of myself from various stages of childhood and young adulthood. As an adult, whenever I saw a photo of myself, I immediately destroyed it, even if other people were in the picture. Of course, I missed a few. Sifting through the pile, I found a picture of myself in front of a birthday cake. I wore a pink polo that I thought made me look more feminine. Tears were in my eyes, my lips were pursed; I looked like a miserable duck. *To each look miserable, we were twin infinitives.* The point is, I myself did not want to exist photographically, and it was very devastating for most people.

Many years ago, my adoptive mother insisted on visiting me at my college dorm in Iowa.

There are no photos of your family, she observed as we stood together in my dorm room.

It was strange to me, the way she said *your family*. The way she said *your family* made it sound like something detached and distant from both of us. She might have been talking about Ethiopia.

Why are there no photos of your family? she asked me. Don't you miss your family?

I tried to explain my position on photography. It's just that a second captured on film doesn't accurately represent the real world, I said to her.

She looked at me as if I were some kind of New Age-y person.

People who call themselves photographers are fake, I went on, the real charlatans of our time. Behind a photo is a perfectly fake person, scrubbed of all flaws, dead inside.

Everyone is attached to photos, I said, and I have no attachment to photos, I never have.

Photos are sentimental, I said, and I'm not a sentimental person.

You're ashamed of your family, she said, you've always been ashamed of your family. What did we do to you, Helen? Why are you so angry with us?

I told her that they had done nothing to me, that they had raised their adoptive children perfectly, that I wouldn't have changed a thing.

You're lying, she said, you've always had a talent for exaggeration and drama. That's the reason you went to college, she continued. To hone your dramatic flair. I'm sorry your father sent you here, I'm sorry your father paid for this.

She gestured around the dorm room.

I laughed because we were both standing in a tiny airless concrete cell.

I'm sorry he paid for it, too, I said, I'm sorry he paid for the cheapest college I got into.

No one wanted to hear about my anger, especially not my adoptive mother. Her face came back to me; in my mind, I saw her mouth shaped into a bird beak. Her hands were on her hips in an exaggerated pose of disapproval. She wore a collared shirt with flowers embroidered on it, a shirt she considered to be dressy, the most appropriate shirt in her wardrobe for a weekend college visit.

A few weeks later, an envelope arrived in my dorm mailbox with nothing in it but a truly grotesque family photo taken by a professional photographer at a department store: my adoptive parents and my adoptive brother smiling vapidly in front of a fake brick fireplace. My adoptive brother's eyes were especially glassy, like a mounted animal specimen. Of course I wasn't in it, and it pleased me to think of them as a unit detached from my own existence. My college roommate Beth watched me tear it up and throw it away.

You've always been a coldhearted bitch, she said with admiration.

16

A POLICEWOMAN WAS at the front door. She was peering in through the window next to the door when I happened to walk through the foyer. I just happened to be walking by, fresh from the toilet, when I saw her peering in rudely. I opened the door, hesitantly.

Hello?

Hello. Is Mrs. Moran in?

I'm afraid not. She's out with the grief counselor.

Okay, dear, what about your dad?

The policewoman seemed to think I was younger than I was, and I couldn't tell if she wanted to be invited in or not.

I'm checking to see if everything's okay, she said.

Because of my activism against the police, now that one was in front of me, in flesh and blood, I wasn't sure how to react. I'm sorry, I've been home the entire afternoon, doing nothing, I said, is there anything else?

Well, she said, this is for your mom. She thrust forward a plate with something wrapped in foil.

Out of curiosity, I accepted it, and shut the door.

I brought the plate into the kitchen and removed the sheet of foil. F O I L is a beautiful word, I thought, almost as beautiful as T I M E. On the plate was a white double-layer cake, frosted. I helped myself to a slice, then another, with a large, hefty bread knife. I brought my plate into the den. I had no idea when my adoptive parents would be back, or for how long the house would be this empty, how long I would feel this stillness spreading out in front of me. How silly it is that we organize life with *minutes and hours and days and months and years*. Time is a human construction, like gender and race and capitalism. I took a few bites of cake. Wild animals don't have a concept of hours, birds don't have a concept of days, not even fish... Suddenly, the house phone rang. It took me a moment to see that it was buried underneath a pile of photos.

Hello? I said cheerfully.

It's Thomas, the voice said, I'm free now.

You were supposed to call me on my cellphone, I said, not my adoptive parents' house phone.

Sorry, do you want to talk now? I just got off work.

Could you meet me somewhere? I said.

Where?

I haven't been back here in years and I don't have a car, so somewhere close by.

I'll come to your parents' house. I know where it is.

I hung up the phone, annoyed by the mess on my adoptive father's desk. Organize yourself! I said to no one. Organize this situation! Simplify this mess! I took a bite of cake. It's always easier to reduce complicated situations to a simple idea. I preferred it that way. I preferred simplicity, seamless boundless simplicity! Timeless elegance! I started to put together the pieces of his suicide arrangement. I flipped through ten more photos. In each photo I found of him, he was frowning or neutral. He was a gentle person; he had never been prone to violence, he always seemed like the docile one, whereas I was the violent one, full of rage, who day after day threatened to destroy the peace.

I stopped looking at photos. I turned on the computer and looked up a few things on the internet. The doorbell rang and I went to answer it. A young man with pale hair appeared on the doorstep. He was probably my adoptive brother's age, maybe a little older. He was wearing his uniform from work, a fast-casual restaurant, and I saw beads of sweat on his brow, his nose. He took off his headset self-consciously and folded it into his pocket. I told him to come in. We went into my adoptive father's study and sat down in chairs facing one another. I took out my traveler kit and popped a couple pills to calm down my thoughts. I offered him a piece of the policewoman's cake, which he accepted. I went into the kitchen and cut two slices. I would eat another piece with him. I did not offer him a drink, as it wasn't that kind of social visit; we were meeting to talk about a suicide, we had come together to look into the *abyss*. I took out a piece of paper from the desk. I wrote down INTERROGATION OF THOMAS.

Where is everyone? said Thomas. Are you always alone in the house like this?

My adoptive parents are out making funeral arrangements and working, I said. They're very busy right now.

I realized my voice had an artificial quality or the tone of a museum docent speaking in front of a large group of children. Let's start over, I said quietly. Thomas, how do you know my adoptive brother?

School, he said, I went to the same school as you. You were a couple grades ahead. You don't remember me? I used to come over to your parents' house with Zachary Moon all the time after school to hang out with him. By the way, I told Zachary, and he said he's going to come home as soon as he can.

And when was the last time you saw my adoptive brother? I asked.

It must have been a week ago, said Thomas. He told me he wasn't feeling well even though we had made plans to have dinner. I picked him up from your parents' house and we drove by our old school. You know the place, you went there, too, it's not far from your house.

It's within walking distance, I said.

Right, said Thomas, your brother wanted to see it and I didn't ask him why. I think it made him wistful and nostalgic. I was hungry and when I suggested we get something to eat, he told me he wasn't hungry, that he didn't want to eat anything.

We ended up going to his favorite Greek restaurant. I was starving and I thought taking him there would help his appetite. When we got to the restaurant he sat across from me in the booth and didn't really say anything. Then I noticed something strange: he was talking with his hand in front of his mouth. Maybe he was embarrassed about something in his teeth. So I didn't say anything. Besides, if something was wrong, I knew he was taking care of it. He was always making appointments with doctors. He was always in and out of a hospital and doctor's appointments, so I figured he was going to take care of it.

What do you mean, I said, that he was always in and out of a hospital?

I guess he was always making appointments with doctors for various things, anyway, that's what he told me, I never went with him to the hospital or doctor, so I don't know for sure, said Thomas. I would ask him what was going on and he didn't want to talk about it. His mouth wasn't bleeding or gross. He just had a strange way of speaking that night. He would put his hand up, or he would sort of pull his lips over his gums. It was very strange.

And what did you do after going to the Greek restaurant? I said.

I took him home, Thomas said. It took him a long time to get out of my car. We were pulled up at the side of your house and the passenger door was open. His feet were out, his legs half out. He stayed that way for a while as we talked. He couldn't make up his mind. In or out, I said. Out, he said. For the next half-hour, he didn't make any motion to leave. Finally, I told him I was really tired and had to go. I sort of pushed him out of the car, not in a violent way, in a very gentle way. Let me try to say it like this: I pushed him out, gently but firmly.

What did you do when you got home? I said.

I fell asleep. I was tired. I called him first thing in the morning, around nine, he told me that he had a nice night out. He said, I had a nice night out with you, thank you for being in my life. I told him he was talking crazily; I asked him if he was drunk. Of course he wasn't drunk, he never drank or smoked or anything. I asked to see him that day, but he said he had things to take care of. I never saw him or heard from him again. I texted him and he didn't text me back. I called and it went to voicemail.

When I called you, how did you feel? I asked.

How do you think? he said.

It was crazy, too, a relative of your parents called me and told me what happened, he said.

I should have known something was wrong, he cried. I think something in his mouth bothered him, but what was it?

You must mean Uncle Geoff called you, I said excitedly. Good old Uncle Geoff as the messenger.

It looked like Thomas was crying, but I wasn't sure, so I kept talking.

A few minutes before you arrived, I was in a state of panic, I was unorganized, and you were about to arrive. Everyone always arrives at the worst possible moment. You were on the doorstep about to ring the doorbell when I looked something up on the internet, I said to Thomas. I went to a mental-wellness website, which I trust as a source, and it states there are six common reasons people commit suicide: 1) they're pathological 2) they're depressed 3) they didn't understand what they were doing 4) they're irrational 5) they have a medical reason 6) they lost control. We must rule out that he was pathological or irrational, and as far as I know he never lost control. He composed his suicide, I said, more than he composed his own life. He was obsessed with planning and preparations, and he left nothing to chance.

Because of what I knew of him and his planning obsession, I said, he absolutely confounded me, his only adoptive sister, when he showed up unexpectedly and out of the blue at my shared studio apartment in Manhattan one day at the end of July. It was the second thing he did that truly astonished me. And at the time, it made me so angry, because what did he think I had to offer him?

17

THREE MONTHS AGO I was in New York City, and chaotic things in my life, like my living situation, began to stabilize. It had been years since I had seen him. We stayed in touch through email, text, etc., but I never went back to Milwaukee, I didn't go home for the holidays, I stopped doing Thanksgiving when I was in my early twenties, Christmas was the next to go. It took me five years to stabilize in New York City. When you move there, people tell you it will take two years, but it took me five. I started my current job over half a year ago. And it's shit. One morning a few months ago, my supervisor blew his whistle and gathered us, supervisors of the troubled young people, in the most disgusting room of the facility, a room filled with piles of flies and mosquitoes and mold-flecked mugs and one grimy window. Everyone was standing in an oval, a great force of pleated khakis and polos. I was looking at my phone discreetly when I heard my supervisor say something about assembling a team to oversee an internal investigation, and as I looked up with great interest, my coworker Michele told me to go make coffee.

My coworker Michele from the first day of training showed me no respect, she treated me as if I were the least important member of the team, the one who isn't a right fit, the one who always scrubs out the toilets the incorrect way, a way they've never been scrubbed and never should be scrubbed; I was a blight on humanity, and somehow she must have inferred that my blight-on-humanity self was once a barista for minimum wage and cash tips at a punk café when I was in college with nothing better to do, because out of the twenty people standing in the oval, she singled me out.

I left the filthy room and went into the employee kitchen. It had been a long time since I had been a barista; fortunately, I remembered exactly how to brew a carafe of French Roast. As the coffee dripped down into the carafe I wondered what exactly had triggered an internal investigation in the first place, I imagined someone violating all of the employee handbook's precepts, all of the rules and procedures we went over in great detail during a two-week unpaid professional development session, and I was certain I myself would never be under investigation, because my infractions were so minor, for example sometimes I took too many bathroom breaks so I could check my phone in peace, or occasionally when I cleaned the bathrooms I shoved the stack of paper towels up through the slit in the dispenser instead of getting the key and opening the loading door and inserting the stack properly.

When I returned to the filthy room with two carafes of French roast, I noticed everyone had dispersed, the meeting was over, and someone had thoughtfully opened the window to air out the odor of too many humans in one room. I left the carafes and returned to my desk deeply embarrassed I had been left out of the meeting. No one bothered to update me, no one sought out my presence or decided to tell me what was discussed. No one even thanked me for making coffee.

Look at what's in front of you, I said to calm myself, that's what matters.

Above my work desk I had pinned several photos of my favorite troubled young people: most of them were gone, some of them went on to community college or for-profit technical schools, some of them went into menial labor and customer service but sometimes all of my troubled young people's faces blurred into one gigantic face of sadness and despair, so I asked the ones I liked for photos, even though I hated photography, simply to be able to remember their individual names and faces, otherwise I would forget. As I sat in silence and reflection, my period began unexpectedly, and bled through my khaki work-pants. I stood up. A giant splotch of dark brown had formed. Michele pointed out the splotch, infuriating me, and she offered to wipe it with a moist towelette. I told her no, and she went ahead and wiped it anyway. After her senseless violation, I could feel the splotch had doubled in size. Michele and the towelette had brought it back to life, and the towelette's scented moisture had soaked through the khakis to my underwear so that I was shivering at my desk, which was situated directly under an air-conditioning vent.

I kept forcing my anger down below my passive surface. The

night before, I went to a party with my roommate Julie in Bushwick, that shitbox of a neighborhood, where a drunk man tried to hold me down and kiss me at three in the morning. I was left with no choice but to bite down on his tongue as brutally as possible. I drew blood, and I felt a piece of his tongue come off into my mouth, a small flap the texture of a gumdrop that I spit out.

She bit me! he screamed, shoving me away. She bit me!

As if he were talking about a rabid dog! There was blood everywhere! I was so angry!

You're not going to put a baby in me, I told anyone who would listen. Sister Reliability doesn't fuck!

I was fine with genitalia in my face and blow jobs and spitting out their sperm, I was fine with rimming, I made my peace with it, and I was so angry. Underneath my peace there was anger, an ugly anger, the force of it was formidable, and I was the one who had to live with it. Everything was bitter.

I had no more interest in sexual relations than I have in the mating habits of cockroaches! I'd rather study flowers for the rest of my life than have sex! I'd rather have my nose in tulips and roses! When my roommate Julie suggested that I might be a closeted lesbian, after she discovered my preference for LGBT novels, I snorted.

A woman on top of a woman is just as disgusting as a man on top of a woman, I said to her, it's all the same to me!

I had a huge stain on my pants. Michele and the moist towelette made the stain worse, she forced the stain to set into the fabric, causing it to look even larger and darker, I saw for myself in the bathroom. If I stood up or walked around the facility, my coworkers would see I had no control over what came out of my body.

I decided to go home early, I told everyone I was sick, then I made plans to meet my roommate Julie's friend Steve for lunch.

He wrote novels and short stories about virgin bachelors from Switzerland who liked to look up women's skirts. I felt a tenderness toward him for his mousy grayish hair, the small, adorable pink pimples above his lip, etc. Perhaps I wasn't gay or straight, perhaps I was *perverse*.

Do you want to get lunch? I would text Steve.

The next thing I knew, he would appear on the sidewalk below my shared studio apartment with a bag of deli sandwiches and pink lemonades with pulp, which we would take to the park and sometimes I would throw my leftover sandwich at the ducks and swans. One time I killed a baby duck, by accident. The heel of bread was harder than I thought. At the time I didn't know my own strength. That early afternoon my shared studio apartment's buzzer would not stop buzzing, and I assumed it was Steve with a sandwich. It was insistent and upsetting. I changed out of my pants and into red Umbros. I tried to buzz the person in, but it didn't work, and the buzzer kept ringing. I ran down the stairs in an agitated mood, only to be shocked by my adoptive brother's appearance out of the blue. It took me a moment to register that it wasn't Steve. I almost said, You're not Steve! To my adoptive brother! I apprehended his figure, slightly hunched and embarrassed. I saw that his brown Korean eyes were like the light reflecting off warm toad-ridden ponds in a dark ecology.

Hello, I said. What are you doing here?

That day something bad happened, then something good. His appearance was like when a character out of a fairy tale appears magically for no reason but to possibly improve the situation. His clothes were wet from the rain, and they smelled slightly worse than typical New York City pollution. He was wearing a New York Yankees baseball cap, and I never understood why he liked them, I didn't ask, I assumed there was a terrible reason behind it, and now I'll never know.

I tried to call you, he said as he stood in the vestibule. I called and called and you didn't answer. Your phone kept ringing. It didn't go to voicemail and my text messages were bounced back.

My phone must have died, I apologized, it must have died in the rain.

That's okay, he said.

Does this sound like someone impulsive, psychotic, and crying out for help? Does this sound like a person who made a mistake?

The next day, I said to Thomas, I received an email from my supervisor informing me that I was being placed under an internal investigation…

18

THOMAS LOOKED DOWN at the floor. He no longer looked sad and allergic, in fact, he looked upset, and I recognized immediately a face of disgust. It was almost like looking into a mirror: the brow furrowed, the eyebrows knit closely together, the lips curled up.

Is something bothering you? I said.

Well. I just don't understand why you felt like you had to tell me all of that. What did any of that have to do with… anything. What did that have to do with anything?

Wait a second. I'm not done. I didn't even get to the good part. There's more.

I should get going. I'm not feeling very well.

He stood up from the chair. I followed his polo shirt out of the den and into the foyer.

Can I still call you if I think of any more questions? I said.

I guess, he said as he put his headset on, but it would be better for me if you didn't.

Why's that? What do you mean by that?

Never mind, said Thomas.

Before he left, he turned around.

It's so dark in your house. Why don't you turn on some lights? It's like you're sitting on top of a pile of darkness. It's not normal. It's really fucking weird.

Then he ran out the front door and down the evenly paved driveway until he reached his car, a small hatchback.

I went around to each room and switched on as many lights as possible. The house did not get sun exposure. Everything inside it died.

In some of the rooms, I pulled open the curtains and a filthy gray light entered. When the light entered, I shut the curtains. Then opened them. Then shut them. Then opened. Then shut. Then opened. Then shut. Then opened. I was finally in a good place, I thought, mentally and emotionally. At one point early in my investigation, I had told myself I needed to inspect my adoptive brother's bedroom with a magnifying glass. Now every time I approached his bedroom door, something repelled me and pushed me back. I finally realized that my attempt to theorize his suicide was a lapse in judgment, and suddenly it disgusted me. There are six reasons, I said to no one. Of course there were more; there were thousands of reasons to commit suicide, six reasons was shorthand for the abyss. And I realized there was a material reality to his death that I had refused to wrestle with.

Was his room a crime scene? I wondered. Did he kill himself in his own room?

If he committed suicide in his room, my adoptive parents would have to sell the house as soon as possible. In no time I exhausted myself as I pictured my adoptive parents putting the house on the market, selling the medieval fortress, which did not come cheaply built. They would put that in the ad, that it did not come cheaply built, and then they would have to show the house to house-hunting strangers, but before that they would have to empty all the knickknacks out of the rooms and pack them into boxes. No, they would have to hire someone to do that type of work, someone cheap, someone foreign with a good work ethic. There's dignity in work, my adoptive father liked to tell us, when there was an us.

I returned to my adoptive father's study where I examined what I had written down when I spoke with Thomas. MISSING TOOTH and DOCTORS, my second clue. I couldn't help but picture him talking with his lips covering his gums and I almost laughed out loud. My near-laughter caused my right temple to pulse and I took out my traveler kit and swallowed a pill for sinus-pressure relief. My adoptive brother always had perfectly shaped, straight white teeth; I was the one burdened with cavities, crooked teeth, loose gums, extra wisdom teeth, teeth growing upside down and to the side, etc. I had never felt at peace with my mouth. And my thoughts returned to the receipt that the balding European man had pointed out to me. Where had I put that?

I tried to picture where I left it when the doorbell rang, disrupting my picturing! I wondered if it would be a deliveryman with my sweater. I was looking forward to wearing the black turtleneck sweater to his funeral. I have always preferred to be in the background, an extra in the movie of my own life, but if people had to look at me at the funeral ceremony, at least I would be wearing a black turtleneck, which would convey a sense of mystery of the abyss. I went into the foyer and before I opened the door, I tried to compose my face, I relaxed my facial muscles so it would look as if I were at peace, I felt my skin loosen, and when everything relaxed into an expression of neutrality, I opened the door. I was astonished to see a person holding not a cardboard box with my sweater, but a basket of flowers and underneath the basket a clipboard. The basket of flowers obscured the person's face. There was a body and a basket of flowers for a head. Sign here, said the creature, and it handed me a clipboard. I scrawled my name and then it gave me the basket. After it gave me the basket, and I set it down in the foyer, it gave me another. There were three more baskets in a row behind the man. It took me a while to bring all the baskets into the house, and some of the flowers of mourning spilled out onto the floor, peace lilies and palm fronds and baby's breath. I thanked the now-human, a very short man with the clipboard, and closed the door with my foot. The baskets were in a row near the grandfather clock and I looked at the tiny cards attached to each of the baskets. From the Grants, one said, your neighbors with deepest sympathy. From the Slothers, all of our regrets. I hoped that the hall filled up with even more flowers, which would be a beautiful thing for my adoptive parents, especially my adoptive mother who loved flowers and every living thing. That would be the silver lining of this catastrophe. I gathered up all of the flowers from the baskets and dumped them into the mop bucket to keep them fresh. Pleased with myself for thinking ahead, I went into the kitchen.

Look for the receipt, I said to no one. Look for the medical bill, I said to the air. I stared blankly at my adoptive mother's desk for a long time, almost as if I had stepped outside of time itself, until I opened the desk drawer and finally saw the receipt or perhaps I should say my brain registered the image of the receipt, as if it were some kind of holy and miraculous object, either way the receipt materialized. It was a page-long hospital bill with a name, DR JONATHAN ABE, address, and phone number in the upper-right-hand corner along with a list of charges for various examinations in some kind of billing code. The date was May 3, 2013. It seemed all of the charges were covered by the insurance. In my hands was a harmless medical bill, which a few months ago meant nothing to anyone, and now it's full of possibility. Meaning accumulates over time, I thought, who could say why?

I picked up the household phone and called the number: a pleasant, automated voice message instructed me to choose from five different options, I pressed "0," hoping to reach a human operator, and the system sent me back to the original message, I pressed "1," which took me to an outgoing message for the pharmacy, I pressed "0" and returned to the original menu. I kept looping back and forth until I had exhausted all five options. No human answered the phone even after pressing "0" multiple times. I hung up the phone. Everything in the house was silent. I stared at the medical bill with its alien code and useless phone number; I wanted to rip it up with great precision because it told me nothing about how he lived, it told me nothing about why he died.

19

I LEFT THE HOUSE for a walk. It was brighter outside. No one rushed about with errands. The houses were empty. I liked to utilize walking as a head-clearing apparatus. I wore a large man's Carhartt sweatshirt with the hood up, jeans, and a pair of Adidas Sambas I found two years ago in Central Park next to a garbage can; each shoe was a different size. I continued past a lawn with a black lawn jockey set out like a warning. For a block I stared at the sidewalk, and almost got hit by a car. I looked up when I heard an SUV honking, the honk stretched out for ten angry seconds. Through the windshield, a woman's face flashed, outraged and terrified. I waved to let the woman know I was okay.

I told myself I would try to literally follow in his footsteps, to see if he had left any clues. I was searching, searching, searching. I went up the hill to the pharmacy. Above the pharmacy was the former home of a child pornographer, right in the middle of town.

I took a picture of it on my phone. My phone pinged. It was a message from my supervisor. He asked me a few questions about particular dates and what I did with the troubled young people. He apologized for asking, he knew I was in the middle of a difficult time.

Down the tree-shaded railroad tracks there was a gourmet grocery store that used to sell a tiny can of tomato paste for ten dollars. He walked the dog along the tracks, when he and the dog were alive, I thought. I tried to see the path through his eyes; I tried to imagine what he thought about. The last time he came here, was he covering his mouth? What did that detail mean?

There were no traces of him or the dog, except perhaps the dog's shit absorbed into the dirt. I crunched across the grass covered over with leaves next to the tracks and pursued the railroad as it snaked past the church parking lot, which made me shiver with disgust. I remembered immediately how I had refused to wear the veil for my First Communion. I wore a bejeweled headband whereas all of the girls in my class put on their veils; none of them had had the courage or strength then to refuse or question what we were constantly forced to do. Stupid white bitches getting married to God!

Most of my childhood memories were situated around acts of refusal, I thought as I walked along the railroad, first refusing the veil, then refusing to go to church and do confession, then refusing to stay in Milwaukee. After refusing to be in Milwaukee, I refused to stay away from Milwaukee and came back, only to go away again. Each act of refusal led me further away from my adoptive family, yet somehow increased my communication with my adoptive brother. As an adult I spoke less to my adoptive parents and more to my adoptive brother. As an adult I learned to accept things as they were, this was another great talent of mine. Some people might call it resignation, but that's not the way I saw it. I understood that it was a very humble and ethical position, perfect for receiving bad news or being deeply disappointed.

I must have taken a wrong turn somewhere, because I was in the middle of an unfamiliar neighborhood. The houses were the size of three houses. I walked on the sidewalk, freshly swept, leaf-free. This street would have made him very uncomfortable. He never said anything about wanting to move out of our childhood home, for him the goal of home ownership would have been impossible since he never had a job or credit. He took a career aptitude test in high school, he told me, and the result was manager. Manager of what? When the guidance counselor asked him what kind of occupation he envisioned for himself, he said lifeguard. At times, he had a sense of humor.

He frequently wrote me letters of complaint about our adoptive parents, and I found it easy to be in relation to him, I enjoyed them even, but as his letters turned to the frustration he was having in locating his biological mother in Korea, I began to feel burdened. You'll never find her, I wrote back to him, because she doesn't want to be found, give it up!

I have always been a great dispenser of advice and was surprised more people didn't consult me or seek me out. Why was I always seeking others out and no one comes to look for me anymore?

I didn't understand his impulse to investigate his biological mother, because I wanted nothing to do with my own biological mother, the stupid whore! The whore fucked and made a baby, I thought, and then the whore gave the baby away. If you're going to fuck, keep the baby, I thought, keep it or abort it. It was that simple. I was not pro-life, I was ambivalent about life; I did not believe that its sanctity was a given, I did not believe life was itself a special privilege. Perhaps my world became too small to contain his complaints and disgust. I had my own complaints and disgust. He wasn't that isolated, I told myself. If he got desperate, he had our adoptive parents to talk to. Now, since I've been at the house and around my adoptive parents, I can see all the gaping flaws of that logic. It's like a piece of Swiss cheese. Fuck. Was there blood on my hands? I wondered. No, I had wiped my hands clean. I had even sanitized them.

If I did nothing for him, at least that's neutral, at least a zero doesn't cause anyone any harm. I had been so lost in my thoughts, I failed to notice a middle-aged man on his front doorstep, glaring at me.

What business do you have here? he shouted. Young man! Answer me now!

He must have been shouting because he was deaf.

I took off my hood. I'm not a man, I said loudly.

What's your name, then?

Helen.

This is a private neighborhood.

I'm sorry to disrupt the peace.

The man didn't say anything and returned to his estate. I'm sorry to disrupt the peace was my stock apology; I used it all the time at my workplace, it was a good apology because it could mean so many different things to people. It could mean, I'm sorry, I made a mistake. It could mean, I'm sorry, I'll ruin you, bitch. On the way home, I stopped at the ice cream parlor. The parlor inside was empty and the cloying smell of sugar and milk overwhelmed me. A woman in a red apron came out from a door behind the counter. I ordered a scoop of vanilla ice cream in a cup. Because my adoptive brother was an occasional customer, I asked the woman if she knew him. I described him, what he looked like, etc. She told me she didn't serve many Asians.

You're the first one in a while, she said.

When I got home, I was so exhausted I drifted past my adop-
tive parents in the second living room. They were listening to
a Beach Boys record, holding each other on the wicker-basket
couch. Why wouldn't anyone admit that a life is not a life but a
deathward existence? I went up to my childhood bedroom, where 7
I took three tablets of sleeping pills plus one of my roommate
Julie's Xanax, and fell into a deep, untroubled sleep.

THE SECOND DAY

20

THE SECOND DAY OF MY investigation I woke up to the sound of the garage door opening and closing. I woke up in an extreme state of anxiety over the things I had to do. Already so much had happened, I learned things, I received information from Thomas, a bounteous source of clues. Put the knowledge to use, I said. Organize yourself! I dressed myself in plain, gray clothes like a warden's, and went downstairs where there were two notes on the kitchen table.

The first one was in my adoptive mother's handwriting: Helen, we both are in meetings this morning. What happened to Pam's cake? It was meant for the lunch reception after the funeral. It looks like you ate all of it. It's 65 degrees out and unseasonably warm.

The second was from my adoptive father:

PAM USED HER SPECIAL RECIPE.
THAT CAKE WAS FOR AFTER THE
FUNERAL, NOT FOR YOU.

I crumpled up the notes; of course that cake had a special purpose! It would be a good time to bake the pie as a response, but I was not a pie baker. I never was. I did not please people, I did not please myself. I noticed a box of pizza had been left out on the counter. Because it was so large and awkward, I took it out to the garbage cans in the driveway. Despite their obsession with organization and tidiness, my adoptive parents never properly stored their garbage cans and recycling bins. They always left them outside and sometimes at night the animals from the woods got into them and they tore apart the food packaging and left it strewn across the driveway. This morning I noticed there were two egg containers, a can of whipped cream, and an empty box of Trojan condoms, which I was sure did not belong to anyone in my adoptive family.

That morning it was unseasonably warm for the beginning of October. There was no one outside walking the dog or running errands. No one watched me. I closed my eyes. It was the beginning of a bright day, and I felt the brightness burn through my eyelids. When I opened them, I looked across the street at a large modern house, a box of glass. Behind the house a relatively unmolested forest spread out, where I never liked to walk or think because when I was a child, there had been rumors of a child kidnapping taking place in the middle of the forest, or perhaps it was said that some kind of ogre-man lived there and kept a little boy as his sex slave, later as I grew older and came to understand those rumors as fairy tales designed to teach children a lesson (don't go anywhere without your parents, don't go off with strangers), I still avoided the forest for the simple reason that I thought the neighbors would see me, as there was a two-story glass wall the length of the house facing the forest. And as far as I knew, my adoptive brother never went into the forest, he came up with all of his ideas, probably even his suicide plans, by pacing back and forth in his childhood bedroom, the main place of rest for him. I stood at the end of the driveway looking out at the forest behind the neighbor's house.

He was not a flexible person, I remembered, and therefore he was very uncomfortable when he visited me in Manhattan. To live in Manhattan one has to be extremely flexible. I turned toward my childhood home. In order to survive in New York City one has to be willing to bend to the city's whims. Bend to the city's whims! I thought. Bend or perish! Sometimes you had to be flexible enough to withstand being trapped underground on a train car in the Bronx at three in the morning after a night of dancing and doing drugs, so said my roommate Julie, or it might mean to take what you wanted when you saw it, wherever you happened to be. I saw that happen often enough, mostly when I observed my troubled young people take what they wanted and I will admit that I did not encourage them and I did not discourage them; I simply looked around and saw a great number of things, I saw the city as a horn of plenty, and after I looked at everything that everyone else had, I thought *why shouldn't* my troubled young people have whatever it is they've taken, *let it be theirs!* When I considered all the things they had taken, I was always shocked at how small and inconsequential everything was. Cigarettes and candy and chips and sunglasses and toys from the hanging-claw arcade game and plastic trinkets made in China that didn't mean anything to anyone.

A squirrel darted out from a bush with a piece of pizza crust in its mouth. The name Zachary Moon came into my brain. Zachary Moon from high school and beyond, what would he have to say? I decided to walk to his childhood house, a house I knew well since as soon as I passed my driver's test, I was forced to drive there every weekend, dropping off and picking up, so my adoptive brother would have at least one male friend. Since I had been home, I thought he had no friends, but that wasn't right.

Get it right, I said to no one. Organize yourself!

Perhaps he had more than two friends. Perhaps Zachary Moon's parents would be home and I could question them. I went through the center of the suburb, and then in the direction of the city. People came out of their houses depressed and went into cars. The Moon house was on the edge of the suburb, right next to a small cemetery. On the way to the Moon residence, I stopped in at a gas station, and bought a pack of cigarettes, a lighter, and a bottle of water. To get to the house I had to walk through the cemetery, which disoriented me in the bright sun. I smoked a cigarette as I went up and down large mounds of grass, and each time I descended one, the gravestones, grand and imposing, overwhelmed me. I smoked another cigarette. It took me over an hour to reach the Moon house, a mini-mansion that housed nine children plus the two parents. There was a rundown tennis court in the front lawn, the net in shreds. I walked up the gravel driveway. I remembered the exact sound the car wheels made when I put the car in reverse. I went to the door and rang the doorbell. I waited five minutes. No one answered. People were at work, I thought. The last time I dropped off my adoptive brother at this house, he and Zachary Moon were smoking cigarettes in the car, which at the time distressed and infuriated me. After ten minutes of meditative thinking and smoking my own cigarettes, I gave up and left.

On my way back toward the cemetery, I ran into what I could only assume were the parents. I startled them out of a leisurely walk through the neighborhood. They were older than I expected and I was shocked to see they were Asian, perhaps Korean. It came back to me that they were the two Asian parents in a mansion on the edge of the suburb. They had converted to Christianity and adopted nine children of various ethnicities and abilities. The friend was white, perhaps with a disability. I stubbed out my cigarette quickly and asked them if they remembered my adoptive brother.

Oh yes, said Mrs. Moon. He was quiet and well-behaved. I really was so thankful he became friends with Zachary.

I told them he recently committed suicide; I began to go over the six most common reasons, and once I got to the part about losing control I noticed Mr. Moon pulling on his wife's arm.

It's not good to talk like this, he said. You're upsetting her. Look at yourself.

21

THEY TOLD ME NOTHING. I hadn't imagined anything, so it was nearly impossible to be disappointed, but still they told me nothing to help my investigation. I wandered through the cemetery, which put me in a philosophical mood, then took the bus, a foul-smelling vehicle, back to my childhood neighborhood. As I approached the house, I noticed the garage door was open. I smoked a cigarette, almost hoping my adoptive parents would come out and ask me what I was doing, what was wrong with me.

Inside the garage, I noticed something out of the ordinary. There was a car, my adoptive brother's car, a cheap black Honda with the 666 license plate that my adoptive mother considered paying an exorbitant sum to have changed, the devil's car, she shuddered, *a Satan mobile*. I looked at it for a while. What was so out of the ordinary was that it was parked in the garage at all, as the garage was for my adoptive parents' cars, the children's cars were always parked in the driveway, now his car was parked in the garage. The car's exterior, freshly washed and gleaming like something out of THE BOOK OF CARS, reflected my disgusting appearance, my eyes looked wide and frightened. The car was unlocked, and as soon as I opened the passenger door, my nose was assaulted by the smell of cleaning disinfectant. For a few minutes, I sat in the front seat, dizzy from the fumes. There was a travel-sized pack of tissues on the floor and several quarters in the cup holder. Other than that, it was in immaculate condition. I got out and slammed shut the door. Looking at his car almost brought a tear to my eye. They'll have to sell it, I said to no one. My adoptive father bought it for him when he graduated high school. There was a lot of tension over whether he would graduate on time. My adoptive father used the car as a way to motivate him to finish high school. It was always like that with my adoptive father. There were always bribes and rewards, even when we were little children, we would make deals with him to get things we wanted. With my adoptive mother we prayed for the things we wanted, and with my adoptive father we bartered. Before I left the garage, I found a spray can of insecticide.

I went into the house and brought the can up to my childhood bedroom, where I sprayed the flowerpot with the red dots. Before I sprayed them, the red dots moved very quickly. It was pleasant to see the spray turn into a white foam that froze the squiggling red dots. I pressed pause on their squiggling; then I ended their lives. It was so enjoyable to have an immediate and visible effect on something, I used up the entire can. All of the flowerpots on the sill were coated in a thick white foam like a man's shaving cream.

Looking at the white foam covering the red dots, I felt something close to sexual desire, the first time in over a year. I went into the bathroom next to my adoptive brother's bedroom, grabbed a towel, went back to my room, locked the door, took off my pants, and rolled the towel into a tube shape and rubbed myself against it as I stared at the clouds of beautiful white foam and thought of a scene from *The Piano Teacher*, when the woman gets out of her overbearing mother's apartment, goes to an adult video store, rents a private booth, and sniffs a tissue. I kept looking at the foam and thinking of the tissue, foam, tissue, foam, tissue. I was on the floor with the towel for an hour. Satisfied, I brushed off the pubic hairs, then folded the towel and returned it to the bathroom. I put my pants on.

The house was as empty as I had left it. More flowers had been delivered and left on the front doorstep. It took me half an hour to bring in all the baskets, amongst three wreaths and five bouquets. The foyer was now full of wreaths and bouquets and cards. I collected all the flowers from their paper wrappers and baskets and placed them into the mop bucket from cleaning the hallway. It was my understanding that standing up in water helped the flowers stay fresh. I looked around for a box with my black sweater, but there were no boxes. The cards were addressed to my adoptive parents, and I noticed I wasn't mentioned in them, it was as if I didn't exist, perhaps because no one had seen me in years, even a few of my relatives forgot me.

To Mary and Paul, went the cards, and it was strange seeing my adoptive parents' names like that, it jarred me into realizing that they were actual people in the world and not everyone had the special, troubled, and difficult relationality as I did with them. To some people, to most people in fact, they were just Mary and Paul. Simple Mary and Paul, Mary and Paul in the Catholic fortress, Mary and Paul with the coupons.

The more I said their names, the more I wondered if they were somehow at fault. It was impossible for me not to connect them to him and his suicide. He lived with them his entire life. Did living with them his entire life somehow drive him to suicide? Perhaps it forced him into depression, which led him to suicide. When someone commits suicide, we must look at the parents first in order to assess where to put the blame, then we can look at the siblings, and after we have examined those relations, we can look elsewhere, at girlfriends and boyfriends, and teachers and coaches, but first we must always begin with the nuclear family unit, we need to examine the intention and force of the members in relation to one another in order to assess the level of guilt and shame appropriate to each survivor-member. I stood in the foyer, paralyzed.

The two living rooms and dining room were brightly lit and if a stranger had walked by a couple hours ago and looked in and observed all the flowers and wreaths and warmth and brightness, he might have felt gladness in his heart, for it was indeed a very sentimental-looking tableau, it looked like something out of Currier and Ives.

Hello? I called out. Is anyone home?

No one answered.

Nothing had changed except the arrival of the flowers, etc.

I went into my adoptive father's study, where I switched on the light, and sat in the chair. It was a leather chair that had an animal smell. I reviewed everything that had happened so far. The main thing that stood out to me was the image of my adoptive brother covering his mouth with one hand while he spoke. I tried to picture his teeth; I knew they were white and nicely shaped, possibly because he was the only one who kept up with his twice-yearly cleanings by the same dentist from our childhood. Our childhood dentist sang songs from the '60s while he cleaned, and scaled, and examined, almost everyone hated the singing, it made going to the dentist unbearable, so even my adoptive mother stopped going. They never found a new one, the idea of searching for a more expensive, professional dentist was unthinkable to them. Better not to go at all, they thought.

I was the only one who didn't mind the singing dentist. What really bothered me about going to my childhood dentist was the hygienist who always had her breasts in my face. She asked me every visit without fail if I had a boyfriend and every time I snorted with disgust. She told me once about her trip to Cancún with her boyfriend, her lover, she called him. I was probably in high school when she started asking whether or not I had a boyfriend and when she talked about hers, I pictured them fucking, which was so nauseating and appalling, I almost enjoyed it.

I turned on my adoptive father's computer and I tracked down the phone number of the dentist's office after a simple internet search. It became very clear to me what I would have to do: I would call the office and ask if my adoptive brother had been a recent patient. If I remembered correctly, the dentist's office always kept immaculate records.

For the first time since I had been home, I knew EXACTLY what to do, I said to no one. When I called the number a receptionist answered pleasantly. I introduced myself and before she could speak, I asked her to picture in her head my adoptive brother, I described for her what he looked like, what our adoptive mother looked like, what I looked like, etc. Start with the physical and then proceed to the mental. I told her in great detail what happened to him, and she seemed utterly shocked.

Oh no, she said, oh no.

The pleasantry drained out of her voice and then there was a distracted silence.

Hello? I said, because I thought she might have hung up.

I'm sorry, she said quickly, I'm here. I'm so sorry.

Then she was silent again.

Do you have his records or not? I said.

We do. I just looked. Although the last time he came here was two years ago. You can have them if you want.

There was the silence again, a vast desertlike silence. What would his records from two years ago tell me? Nothing, I shuddered, except that he always had perfect teeth. Then the receptionist must have handed the phone to a new person, because a different voice came on, a lower, more masculine voice with a pleasant cadence.

Ms. Moran, it said, if you're at your parents' home, and you want to get a cleaning, we can squeeze you in this week. Just let us know. We'd be happy to squeeze you in.

22

OF COURSE I DIDN'T WANT to be squeezed in, I hated to be squeezed, physically or metaphorically, it didn't matter. I stopped caring about my teeth around the time I stopped caring about my skin. I'm sure I had a mouth full of calcium decay. A lot of people have it, I thought, and some have it even worse.

I pictured the dentist's office: a small building that looked like a halfway house, cramped sweaty rooms with hot plates, bachelors in undershirts sitting on beds covered with moss. I would walk or have someone drive me there, and the next thing I knew, I would have his records in my hands. But of what importance was it? What would dental records from two years ago tell me about his suicide?

My stomach rumbled; I went into the kitchen and opened the refrigerator. What was I doing in such a large and extravagantly empty house? I found a red apple at the bottom of the crisper drawer. Its skin was waxy and shining; it looked like an apple from a fairy tale. All humans have an inflated sense of ego, I thought, except the ones who commit suicide, in fact, they have the exact opposite problem, *no ego at all*. I took a bite of the apple, then another. I was chewing the apple thoughtfully when I bit into something soft with a very fine granular texture. I spat it out into my hand: pieces of a black worm. Of course the apples in my adoptive parents' refrigerator would be mealy and filled up with worms, I thought as I entered the study, it made perfect sense for this disgusting house. I considered calling the cleaning woman, but I knew better, I knew that extra cleanings were not calculated in my adoptive parents' monthly budget, already thrown off balance because of the funeral costs, etc. I threw away the rest of the apple into the trash can next to the desk. I noticed it was filled to the brim with wet balled-up tissues.

There was information in my memory, I was certain, I knew there had to be clues buried there, signs and clues pointing toward his death, and it was uncomfortably close to the moment in which I found myself, the moment of sitting alone at my adoptive father's desk in his wood-paneled study, the post-suicide phase. It was easier to fantasize about other things, any kind of thing whatsoever, anything to distance myself from the last time I saw him, I could even think about an octopus wearing a hat, I thought, and I could think about a person wearing an octopus as a hat. I opened my traveler kit and stared at its oblong and bumpy shape. It looked like a tan pill, water-bloated.

It was too easy to picture him, it would've been easier if I hadn't seen him at all, it would've been easier to have only very old memories of him, not new and fresh ones. It was too easy to picture his light blue polo shirt, his damp forehead and his thin dark hair, his slightly thick wrists and fingers, the pore-less skin of his nose and cheeks. Now it seems every memory I have of him, new and old, must be seen, scrutinized, and apprehended through a critical lens, *the lens of his suicide*.

I had already performed the hard and necessary work of understanding him, mostly through his letters and emails, etc. He had already told me everything he wanted me to know. My adoptive brother was a reserved person. He never left the country, he didn't play sports, he talked to my adoptive parents and to people like Thomas, he watched movies and professional sports on his computer, he kept a desk fan running in his bedroom for background noise. He liked quiet things and the fan must have soothed him and it must have soothed him to watch one of the hundreds of movies he first purchased on DVD, then pirated off the internet, I thought as I sat in my adoptive father's study, and yet all the soothing in the world couldn't keep him from killing himself. Did he put a bullet down his throat or into his temple? Did his skull shatter? Was there blood and pieces of brain? Did he hang himself? Did his neck snap? Twenty-nine years old and gone! You should subject your body to physical stress, I once wrote to my adoptive brother in a letter, or your body will decay. Some amount of stress can be good for you. For him, the stress of being alive was enough. Being alive was a contest of endurance for him: how long could he keep himself alive on this planet? I should have told him about The Waterfall Coping Strategy, I thought with regret.

I never looked at him and said, Adoptive brother, what is your existence like on this planet? He never told me anything about himself, and that was certainly part of his plan. In hindsight, I am sure he was covering up a grand scheme, the grand scheme of his suicide. He would have been a great architect, I despaired, or a writer. If he had stayed alive, he would've written long and complicated books that traveled far into the future and past, I was certain. I leaned back in the chair. Doubtless he was a great inventor and fabricator. He was a highly skilled *embroiderer*.

23

HE DID NOT FORM physical relationships, he did not dream of women or men, he did not care to reproduce children, he did not care to go to museums, he did not care for flowers, he did not care to listen to music, especially not music, anything but music. He told me he was *not an active listener,* that he never cared for music, it never interested him, and after I forced him to listen to *Bitches Brew* by Miles Davis 1970, in my shared studio apartment, after listening to the entire thing, and then listening to it again, he changed his mind.

Eye-opening, he said.

Perhaps that was the one helpful thing I did for him that stayed that way. There were no negative repercussions. I asked him if he was interested in seeing live jazz somewhere, even though I had no idea where that would be.

There's so much to see and do in New York City, he said. I spent two weeks debating whether or not to come. I couldn't decide if I should stay in New York City or travel even farther out into the world, a world I have difficulty imagining. It's a pastime of mine to pretend most of the world doesn't exist, and I'm fine not going anywhere.

Planning the trip to New York was a trial. Going through with it was a potential disaster. He told me he waited for the situation to feel perfectly right, that for two weeks he sat at his desk in his childhood bedroom and deliberated over all the possible outcomes for a trip to New York City and beyond. He studied flight maps and schedules, he did research on commercial airplanes and airports, JFK or LaGuardia. He thought he was so smart and prepared. It took him two weeks exactly to come to a feeling of certainty and as soon as he arrived at his decision and booked his one-way ticket to New York City and beyond, he began to feel unsure he had made the correct decision and therefore spent five hours on the phone with various airline customer-service agents going over the possibility of canceling the flights and getting a refund on his credit card.

We are both very indecisive people, he told me. We never learned how to decide anything. Make a list of pros and cons, make a list of possible outcomes, that's what I learned how to do. It's easier to stay at home and yet here I am.

And are you planning on staying with me?

Of course.

He was sitting up on my bed and I sat on the floor.

Where else would I stay?

My shared studio apartment was simply one curtain-divided room with a galley kitchen and no closets and no bathroom and a series of small windows that must have looked like the saddest portholes of a ship going nowhere; my apartment building had more in common with the most run-down boardinghouses of depressing German novels from the 1920s, like a tenement slum, the bathroom was across the hall, every time you went to the bathroom, you had to take a tiny key to get in, sometimes it would take hours to locate the tiny key, and the entire building was unlike any place a normal person would choose to live in the year 2013.

I like your apartment, he said, it suits you.

The one thing I was proud of was my display of found objects on the wire shelf near my bed, things I've found on the street, or stolen, nothing worth more than ten dollars. There were three animal figurines carved out of macadamia nuts, a faded drawing of Marcel Duchamp printed off my roommate Julie's printer, one Swiss Army knife, a glass finch, an old-fashioned amber-colored pharmacy bottle with a skull and bones, a broken record player with assorted broken acetate records, a packet of Genmaicha tea, a skeleton key, a can of pepper spray, tampons, overnight-sized pads, a worn-down biography of William H. Prescott, an SH-50 microphone with no cord, a Japanese NOH mask, one gold Zippo lighter, a giant, heavy fork. It stopped raining, and the sun shone in a friendly way through my apartment window. Directly across from the window there was another building, a shabby concrete affair. So next to the window I had taped a painting of pink flowers. The title might have been SUNLIGHT STREAMING THROUGH PINK FLOWERS, and it reminded me of nature, that it existed, because there were times I forgot. I noticed my adoptive brother staring at it.

It's a French Impressionist. I forget which one.

Our mom has that exact picture in her closet.

I don't think so. I've never seen it.

Yes, she does. Next time you're home, go into her closet. It's above the jewelry box.

I thought he was imagining things, and I suggested we take a walk. Despite our differences, we were both lifelong walkers. We both rejected Catholicism and its pedophile priests and lesbian nuns and took up walking as our religion. Our adoptive parents never walked unless they had to, they drove their station wagons and SUVs to and fro, out of the garage and into another garage, never coming close to nature, avoiding nature at all costs, whereas my adoptive brother and I both from a young age gravitated naturally toward walking everywhere in nature whenever possible, except the forest behind the neighbor's house, the forest that had been forbidden to both of us, the forest of abuse and child molestation and kidnapping, therefore that forest was off limits when we were young for our walking purposes, only later would we be able to walk in the child-molestation forest, and by then we no longer cared to walk there, we each had our own routes of where we liked to walk, he in Milwaukee and I in New York, each of us fixed in habit, each of us unable to take a radical step and alter our ways, until—

I suggested we go to Prospect Park in Brooklyn to sit and walk only because it was more peaceful than Central Park. And now, as I sat in my adoptive father's study, it occurred to me: why didn't I take him to Central Park? Why Prospect Park and not Central? It didn't make sense; I should have taken him to Central Park, I said to no one. Why decrepit and rundown Prospect Park and not Central Park? Tears came to my eyes and I kept saying things to no one as I began to slowly weep.

If you knew someone was going to die a few months later, you would take him to Central Park, not Prospect. It tormented me, the thought that I would never be able to show him glorious Central Park, Central Park in early autumn, Central Park with a scarf and hot chocolate, Central Park with the pigeon people, the golden-hued leaf-draped Central Park of film and TV! That afternoon in July we proceeded down the seven flights of stairs and into the beautiful New York City streets filled with garbage and all kinds of miserable and neurotic people. Sister Reliability! some voices called out, and I thought I saw a few people I recognized as my troubled youth, their faces were distorted with laughter and amusement. I waved back warmly. My adoptive brother and I walked past numerous bodegas and stores that sold wigs and wigs only, we went into a Duane Reade so he could buy cough drops, we descended two flights below ground level into the subway, Dante's inferno. He rushed in through the turnstile behind me. He was a small person and pressed himself easily into my back. Was that the last time he touched me? I wondered. Was that the last time he touched *anyone*? I believed to this day that my adoptive brother never had sex. He was not a sexual person and neither was I. Sometimes I wondered if our lives would have been easier for us if we had both been adopted into an Amish family.

When we got off the train, we walked four city blocks to the park. We came upon a small zoo within the park. He paid for my ticket. Near the zoo entrance a fake-looking cave housed a fat, densely furred cat with short, flat ears and an unhappy, evil expression on its face. We sat down on the iron bench and some men walked by pushing carts selling popsicles and hot dogs. No one looked at us because we were short, miserable Koreans. The zoo was mostly empty. Not even public schoolchildren came to this zoo, it was that depressing. At least it was a bright day. Neither of us pursued the idea of going deeper into the zoo.

I told them I had to go to Wyoming for some job training, he said, but I'm here with you. Can you believe they believed me? I told them I would live at an extended-stay hotel, training with a group of federal investigators. Can you imagine me actually doing something like that? They don't really understand anything about who I am.

That's right, I said sympathetically, they've never understood either of us.

I've come to peace with it. Don't say anything to them.

You have nothing to worry about. I never like to talk to them and it's not like I'm going to start talking to them any time soon.

The truth is, he said, I've started working with a Korean professor at Marquette, Dr. Kim.

Oh?

I tried to act interested, but any time he mentioned Korea, I started to think about other things, particularly a rich person's heavy fork I found in a dumpster in Tribeca a few days ago, a fork that must have weighed ten pounds, with tines that began the width of a finger and tapered into a tiny pencil point, a fork that I thought would be fun to show Steve.

I've been working on it for a few months, he said.

Working on what? I said.

Korean history, he said. I don't go to Marquette, but she told me I could audit her classes. And since I started auditing, I'm helping her out with her research.

That's nice, I said.

I'm at the library all the time, he said, it's a very nice place.

That makes sense, I said. Are you happy with everything?

No, he said, I'm never happy.

He told me the happiest time for him was a period after he graduated high school. He lied to our adoptive parents, he said he had found a job in Madison registering gun licenses. He didn't qualify for any apartments, he had no credit or work history, so he ended up sharing a room in a halfway house. The manager took pity on him. It's funny he lived in a halfway house, because he never drank or did drugs. The manager thought he might be a good influence on his clients. The young man who shared the room with him was a recovering heroin addict.

It was the happiest time in my life, he said, I just went to movies all day, and for money I took surveys online. I didn't have to think about anything.

And no one knew about this? I said.

I had nothing there, he said, and it didn't matter. It was a place you could have nothing and exist. But now I'm working on Korean history, so things are interesting again.

Very nice, I said. I'm glad interesting things are happening.

He laughed a little and then his slight laughing turned into coughing. Like me, it seemed he had a persistent cough throughout the day. He coughed so much it was difficult to understand him at times, because unlike most people, he would try to talk through his cough. As his coughing abated, he asked me who my favorite person was. At the time, I wondered if that was his awkward attempt to find out if I was in a relationship, or dating.

There was a fifteen-year-old girl who I thought had a bright future, full of possibilities. Her name was Isa F., she had brown clear eyes, dark hair always covered up with a black hoodie, and she was a bit of a smart-ass. She sounded like a chain smoker. I was informed her mother was dead, her father absent, an aunt raised her, and that she herself was on her way to becoming an alcoholic. My first day on the job, I noticed her right away, she appeared to know what was actually going on, and what needed to happen, more than the other troubled people. It looked like she was telling other kids to shut up, and even my coworkers appeared to listen to her.

My name is Helen Moran, I said to her.

She looked me up and down. Fuck off, she said.

She reminded me of myself when I was her age, so she was my favorite.

24

I MIGHT HAVE BEEN troubled slightly by his lie about training with federal investigators, but then I remembered I dismissed it just as quickly. Whatever he tells them is none of my business, I had thought. He always lied to them; I could trace his pattern of lying behavior back to when he was ten years old when we played CONFESSION. It never occurred to me to *intervene*. I could be described as many things, but I was not an *intervener*, especially not when it came to my adoptive brother and his life, and perhaps the truth was I was afraid of intervening, because to intervene would mean to communicate with and confront my adoptive parents, people I hadn't looked at in the face for years, perhaps because I was afraid of their faces and always had been. It was easier for me to turn the other way when it came to his lies, and at the time it was much more comfortable for me. I always exploited people and situations for my own comfort.

I was finished with my weeping. Perhaps if I had taken him to Central Park instead of Prospect Park we would have had an in-depth conversation about what was going on in his life, his struggles and worries, his hopes and dreams, but because I took him to Prospect Park, we sat in silence most of the afternoon at the zoo until the sky darkened and it was time to leave.

25

I WAS ASLEEP ON the couch in the study, dissolved in a dream, when my adoptive father burst into the room, terrifying me. He never knocked on doors, or if he did, he never waited for a response, it was his house, he could burst into any room he liked, all of the doors were his to open, none of them came cheaply built. Throughout his life, he burst into rooms and scared people. It was his trademark, I thought, and I'm sure people would talk about it at his funeral.

Helen, you didn't hear us.

Hello, I didn't know anyone was at home.

We've been here for a while. Why didn't you hear us? We were calling out for you and you didn't answer. We kept calling for you, Helen, where are you, your mother called out twenty times. What are you doing in here?

Just looking at family photos.

So you were in here all day, sitting in the dark?

I took a walk. A bright day to the edge of the suburb. I walked through the cemetery to get to the Moon residence, I thought no one was home, then as I turned around and walked away, I ran into the parents. Do you remember them? They were Asian and Christian, much older—

My adoptive mother poked her head into the den.

The food's here, she said.

My adoptive father wasn't listening to anyone. I watched him select several pictures of my adoptive brother, including the birthday picture, and slide them into a manila envelope. I followed him out into the kitchen, where two brown boxes of pizza sat on the counter. Pizza again, I thought, no one had the energy to cook. My adoptive mother was seated at the table, and in front of her was a single slice of pizza on a plate along with a large wedge of iceberg lettuce and a small pool of ranch. I helped myself to three slices.

Do you have any friends you want to invite to the funeral? asked my adoptive mother.

You must have at least one person you could invite, added my adoptive father.

They were always concerned about whether or not I had friends, even for a funeral.

You should bring a friend or two, I heard my adoptive mother say.

Bring them for what? I said.

Then I forced myself to eat the pizza and in my mind I calculated that if I ate three hearty slices, I would be able to skip breakfast and lunch the next day.

As a support, she said, and a comfort.

I don't have any friends I want to call, I said, and I'm very comfortable with that.

Did you know the police were here a couple days ago? said my adoptive mother. They rang our doorbell at three in the morning. I opened the door and they were there. At three in the morning.

Her hands shook as she brought the pizza up to her mouth. It was kind of like watching a very old senile woman eat, and it made me feel terrible; I changed the subject.

Did you see all the flowers and cards from the other people? I asked them. I put them into the buckets to keep them fresh.

Goddammit, Helen, said my adoptive father. He put his pizza slice cheese side down onto his plate.

Yes, of course you did, said my adoptive mother.

She seemed exceptionally calm.

I had to take them out of the buckets, she said. You see, Helen, there was almost a liter of bleach in those buckets. I'm surprised you couldn't smell it. There was more bleach than water, so you actually killed all of the flowers in the buckets in the shortest amount of time imaginable. All of those beautiful flowers in the baskets and paper cones are dead. Luckily, we still have the wreaths, which are lovely. We can use those for the funeral.

She always looked at the bright side of things, I thought.

It's really a shame, hissed my adoptive father, that we had to throw away all of those once-beautiful flowers. In fact, from now on, Helen, you shouldn't do anything in the house without asking us first. You will ruin everything, and the worst part is, you won't even know it. You've already ruined so much. We've been taking care of it all. We don't want you to do anything!

Of course, Chad Lambo has been helping, too, said my adoptive mother, give him some credit, Paul.

I must have frowned because she looked at me and said, What are you thinking about, Helen?

No one had asked me a question like that since I had been home; I took a deep breath, then I told her that I was concerned about the nature of the funeral. When pressed for more details, I went on to say that I didn't think my adoptive brother would want a Catholic funeral.

Of course he does, said my adoptive mother with emotion, I mean, he did. He went to church with us every week. He even liked the priest, Father Luke, a lot. This is what he would want. I'm sure of it.

I wasn't persuaded. How can you be so certain?

I searched their faces, which were pale underneath the light suspended above the table. No one responded. It was silent except for the sounds of their chewing. Sometimes silence can be implemented as a rhetorical strategy. I decided to start asking the difficult questions.

How can you know what a dead person wants or needs? I said. Did he tell you? Did he leave instructions behind? How can you be so certain? Did he leave a suicide letter?

What do you mean by all of that, Helen? said my adoptive father. We knew him very well.

That's not what I meant, I said. I didn't mean you didn't know him really well.

He spent more time with us than anyone else on the planet, said my adoptive father. He spent more time with us than you and now you're suggesting that we didn't know him at all.

Out of the corner of my eye, I noticed the European man helping himself to a slice of pizza at the counter. He made eye contact with me and shook his head.

I'm sorry, I said, I think there's been a misunderstanding. Don't you understand what I'm saying? Don't you understand?

In between asking them if they understood what I was saying, I took bites of my pizza. The tomato sauce and cheese scalded my tongue and ripped off pieces of skin from the roof of my mouth.

It's okay, said my adoptive mother, it's okay, Helen.

It's just us, she said. It's just us.

It looked like she was about to start weeping, so I excused myself and went up to my childhood bedroom where I shut all the windows I had thrown open earlier but not before I looked out at the grim trees. To calm myself, I went into the closet and brought out *The Odyssey*. I read the story of the Cyclops ten times before I closed my eyes in peace. Suddenly the Cyclops occupied part of my brain, and I felt a deep kinship with him. He was misunderstood as a villain, I thought, when in reality, Odysseus and his crew should be positioned as the evil colonizers, and the Cyclops as the dehumanized victim of their atrocious conquest. I've always identified with the victims, I identified with the underdogs, the colonized, the beggars and peasants, the bacteria in the sponge, the mosquitoes and the ants. I would get my revenge one day. Revenge on whom? someone might ask.

I'll show you, I said to no one.

The ones who overlooked me my entire life, all the people who underestimated the power of my will, my life-force.

THE THIRD DAY

26

I LINGERED AT the bottom of the stairs, then shook myself out of a morning paralysis and entered the kitchen. My adoptive mother was at the kitchen table, as if she had never left. She had a pencil behind her ear, and her head was bent down as if she was concentrating deeply on something.

Helen, what's a four-letter word for butter?

There are two sides to everything, I said.

His death on one side, I thought, the morning ritual of the crossword puzzle on the other. When I asked her what she wanted to do that day, she said pray, she wanted to be left alone to pray.

All day? I said.

Before she answered, I went into the empty study. I considered taking a nap in the chair. Everything had been organized; the surface of the desk was clean and smooth. My roommate Julie texted me to remind me that I needed to mail her a rent check. I got up and returned to the kitchen where I heated up a potpie in the microwave for myself, a disgusting, glue-like potpie, which appealed to me in the moment, but I knew I would regret it later. I passed my adoptive mother in one of the living rooms. She sat in a wicker-basket chair with her eyes closed and her palms on her knees as if she were meditating. I brought the potpie with me into the study and sat at the desk. I leafed through a few drawers until I found a box of checks. It's all the same money, I thought, isn't it? I wrote a check to the landlord and slipped it into an envelope, which I addressed with a careless scrawl. It didn't seem like my adoptive father kept very good track of his finances anymore, which was strange because saving money had once been so important to him. I only knew he didn't keep good track because when I asked my adoptive brother how he could afford to fly to New York City since he didn't have a job, he told me he had cashed a couple of my adoptive father's checks that he had written out to himself. He told me he had an entire box of our adoptive father's blank checks in his possession. If my adoptive father knew about it, he never said anything.

I ate my potpie with thoughtful bites. My adoptive brother and I had this in common: we were both prone to being careless with money as a concept and as a vital material. I could never afford my rent with my part-time job helping troubled young people; I relied partially on a small monthly amount from my adoptive father's parents, both dead, the Bach-abusing schizophrenics, which my adoptive father sent to me reluctantly, and I refused to feel badly about it, because there were times when those Bach-abusing schizophrenics were also emotionally and verbally abusive toward my adoptive brother and me, sometimes they had said very inappropriate things to us, especially my adoptive grandfather, especially around the holidays, he would really get into it, first he would hand us each a crisp one-hundred-dollar bill, fresh from the mint, and before we could thank him, he called into question why the two of us had been adopted when there were millions of starving orphans roaming the streets of Korea and eating out of garbage cans.

Why you and you, he would say, pointing at each of us, why the two of you in particular, what's so special about you?

And he seemed to especially enjoy verbally abusing my adoptive brother.

Little man, he called him, and not in an affectionate way.

Small hands, he said shaking his head. You know what they say about boys with small hands.

For some reason, I escaped most of his wrath, although when I graduated college, he told me if I didn't start to have babies I would get uterine cancer.

I didn't feel any qualms about cashing his small monthly checks because all I did was keep myself alive with the bare necessities, the staples, the basics. My ultimate purpose was always to simplify my life, to keep it as small as possible. The first thing you can do to contain your life is to just stop buying things. I almost never purchased anything, not even health insurance. The black turtleneck was a $20 extravagance. While living in New York City, I learned to wear clothes left on the sidewalks of all the richest neighborhoods like SoHo and the West Village. I learned how to alter pants and shirts with a sewing needle and thread. The last time I bought brand-new shoes that fit, I turned twenty-five. I wore shoe sizes from 7 ½ to 11, men's and women's.

I liked to stuff socks into the toe to make them fit and I always had blisters, but I was never uncomfortable.

Walking has always been a huge part of my mental process, I thought as I sat in the chair.

If I can walk, I can think, I thought.

I always had enough money to live on and I never had enough time to live, whereas time was never of any concern to my roommate Julie and her lifestyle. It was strange to live with someone who had so much time for every whim, every impulse, even artistic ones. I, too, once had artistic impulses, I thought, but then they died away. A few weeks ago, she told me she was leaving for a week to take cooking classes in Mexico. She wanted to rediscover her love for cooking. I enjoyed when she left on these little excursions, because it was almost as if I had a normal-sized apartment to myself, even though there was no time to enjoy that space and freedom, I had almost no time for anything when I wasn't at work, I never had time for anything but answering phone calls from my troubled young people. I talked to them all the time; when I was supervising them on the clock, I talked to them about their troubles at home, and when they went home, I had to talk to them on the phone about the troubles they had with other supervisors, my coworkers. They swallowed up countless hours, my hungry troubled young people. Even though it was a part-time job, it took up almost sixty hours a week. That's why they call me Sister Reliability, I thought, I'm always there.

Ever since the suicide, I had set up an auto-reply for my email. To put it plainly, I copied and pasted the content of the email to my supervisor. Of course it's not necessary to subject yourself to such exhaustive work practices, because I believed it was possible to live on nothing in the city and still survive like the cockroaches and rats. It's about knowing the right people, the rich ones, or the friendly ones, and listening to their problems. In fact, I once wrote and designed a FREE PAMPHLET out of my own goodwill, specifically for my troubled young people, titled *How to Survive in New York City on Little to Nothing*.

27

HOW TO SURVIVE IN NEW YORK CITY ON LITTLE TO NOTHING

—

BY HELEN MORAN, 2013

THERE IS A MAN WHO worked all his life to be a success, but everything he touched turned to ashes, and he ended up in the soiled crevices of a corner of the subway, with nothing but a cardboard box and a shopping cart. He didn't even own a *good* broom. There is a woman who has in her possession a bedsheet, some wooden clothespins, a bath mat, and a radio; late in the evening, she walks to a café in the West Village. Outside the café is an empty rectangular cement patio. Eventually, tables and chairs and umbrellas will overtake the patio, but they are locked up inside the café. For the time being, the patio is empty. The woman sets out her bath mat and radio. She makes a tent with her sheet. She uses her imagination to see it as her temporary home, a very beautiful place, filled with promise, until the café manager arrives at six in the morning to discover the woman and her belongings, set up like a refugee camp. The manager tells the woman to find a different place to set up, but not before complimenting the woman on the bath mat.

I have the same one in my apartment bathroom, says the manager.

The most basic thing it behooves you to understand is that, as a poor troubled brown person, rich white people's problems are much larger and more important than yours. If you understand this when you interact with them, and listen to rich people patiently, sometimes they will buy things for you. Or if you happen to not be good with people, but are on friendly terms with a more outgoing and charming person who is poor, you can connect to the rich people through the charming and poor person, because rich people love nothing more than to befriend a group of friendly and poor people, it gives them credibility. It makes them feel noble.

Remember to be interesting. Don't be nice. Nice is not interesting. Nice is the *how are you* of greetings. Nice is the declawed cat, the beige house with the gazebo, and what's the point of a gazebo? An investigative and probing spirit will give you a tour of the boarded-up and condemned house that every rich white person keeps inside herself.

* * *

Once you befriend them, as you get to know them, you can begin to ask for things. First, establish your friendly relationship with the rich person and then after it has been established, say over the span of a couple weeks to a month, you can ask them to buy things for you. This is called ASKING. Create a story designed to pull on their heartstrings. Tell them your feet hurt from your worn-out shoes, which your mother never replaced because she was busy turning tricks, and last night you had a dream in which you miraculously discovered a pair of brand-new shoes underneath your bed. Tell them you have never seen the ocean, and you would like to go swimming in the ocean before you die, but you own no swimsuit or goggles, not even a beach towel in your possession. Ask and receive! Ask and receive! Ask and receive!

A young woman moved from borough to borough. Every time she moved, she kept nothing and slept on the floor of every apartment she ever inhabited in New York City, except her most recent studio apartment, which she shared with a roommate, because the previous roommate left behind a twin bed with a floral bedspread. The mattress was infested with bedbugs, she discovered quickly, the box spring, too. The first month of living in the studio apartment, each morning she woke up with dark red welts up and down her arms and legs and around her torso. Some of them she scratched and infected. Her roommate's body was unscathed, whereas her own body became nothing but a canvas for these welts. She woke up in the middle of the night with a flashlight spotlighting the bed, searching for the blood-sucking parasites, but they were too small, at times nearly invisible. She only saw tiny black specks, *their shit* according to the internet. During the day, if she slid a credit card into one of the ripped seams of the mattress, the bedbugs would flow out in great numbers as if the mattress were stuffed with nothing but the brown-and-red leaf-shaped bugs. For a day, she prayed they would leave. After almost thirty years of not praying, she asked God to take the bedbugs away. When that didn't work, she tried to see things from the bedbugs' point of view. Wouldn't the bugs say to one another, *She's great, but we've had enough, it's time to eat the blood of a new person*?

One bright and sunny day, she decided to take matters into her own hands. She researched how to exterminate them, she bought a toxic powder, and a mask, and sifted the toxic powder over her mattress and into the cracks in the molding, and the electrical sockets. While the toxic poison covered her twin bed with a fine powder, she went on the train to get out of her apartment. A young man sat across from her on the C train, and he kept making eye contact with her, as if he wanted to ask her something. They started talking. It turned out he was a single parent, he did shifts at the co-op, he took the train five stops and a transfer and a ride on the bus to buy his groceries, and he lived in a Crown Heights brownstone. He told her his favorite thing to do was to go to music festivals and casinos, but now that he had a daughter, casinos and festivals were off limits. After they got off the train together, she offered him a bag of harmless drugs she discovered in a locked storage closet at her place of work, in exchange for a place to stay. She explained her situation, she showed him the welts all over her body. She lifted up her shirt and showed him the belt of bites around her waist, then she gave the man a bag of light beige powder the size of a pillow for a tiny dog. Even though he had a daughter, she felt whatever he chose to do with the powder was his business, he was an adult, and it was not in her jurisdiction to police his usage of drugs, illegal or not. She needed a clean bed to sleep upon and the man had offered her a place in his bedroom, in his very own king-sized bed, a bedbug-free paradise-refuge.

Where will you sleep? she asked him. Are you going somewhere?

He had a large duffel bag slung over the shoulder and a small suitcase on wheels.

I'm headed to a casino in Jersey, he said, you'll keep an eye on my daughter, right?

All of this trouble for a clean, bedbug-free bed, she said to him.

In summary, she took a bag of drugs from work and exchanged it for a clean bed. To put it plainly, she had no right to exchange the powder for the clean bed, as the powder was not technically hers, a powder that turned out to be heroin, a missing powder that caused chaos in the upper management of her nonprofit organization, and a missing bag that brought out the police and a detective.

Unfortunately the man from Crown Heights never came back. The young woman stayed in the apartment with the man's daughter for two weeks, until it was arranged for the daughter to live with a relative in California, and when the woman returned to her own apartment, the bedbugs were gone. In a way, it might be said, they all won.

The moral of the story is do whatever you have to do, but first do no harm!

New York City, a city so rich it funds poetry, also has the financial resources necessary to help people get back on their feet, but I want to suggest A NEW WAY, a radical approach without the intrusion of nonprofit organizations, the government, and people, who, though well-meaning, have never walked a day in your shoes.

Less than a year ago, I slammed my compass down and ethical shards flew everywhere. Those shards, when they were whole, did nothing for me! They were better as shards! I swept them up in a dustpan and threw them away. During times of desperation, one's moral compass can shift, in fact, it can be *radical* to alter one's ethical position. Ethical positions should never be laid in concrete, sometimes it's necessary to shift one's moral compass, and sometimes it's necessary to *destroy* it.

28

I MADE HUNDREDS of copies of my pamphlet after I convinced a coworker to show me how to print them on our facility's laser printer. I left them on subway trains, I gave them to people on the street who looked upset, I dropped them off at Marxist bookstores and vegan cafés. One day I helped an elderly Jehovah's Witness down the steps of the A train station, and even though I was running late for work, I gave him one of my pamphlets; if one person could be helped by my pamphlet it would all be worth it.

I was so proud of it, I sent a copy to my adoptive brother, I took great care addressing the envelope, I signed my name extravagantly in green pen. After I sent it to him, he went out of contact for a month. When he came back into communication he never said anything about my pamphlet. I thought he would appreciate me sharing it, I assumed he would consider it a thoughtful gesture, as he enjoyed reading. I never forgot that he liked to read nonfiction thoroughly and in one sitting, and when we were young our adoptive parents thought we both read too much and that we needed to go out into the world more often to interact with the living. When he was in ninth grade his favorite book was about trees, *Drawings of Trees in the Midwest*, it's possible he liked reading about trees because they spent their entire lives in continuous peace. He took *Drawings of Trees in the Midwest* everywhere he went, even to high school where hateful and disgusting kids made him a pariah for carrying around a book about trees. Eventually the book's binding came apart and he threw the entire thing away. I was surprised at his lack of respect for an object that once gave him so much joy; he told me it didn't matter, he didn't need the book anymore, he had memorized the contents and he could see the trees precisely etched and shaded in his mind any time he wanted to, and I didn't understand it, that he would want the trees inside his brain like that, why would he fixate on trees, it didn't make sense. I myself had no particular interest in trees.

29

ONE DAY OUR adoptive father picked us up from school. I was a senior so it was very embarrassing to see him waving at us from the car. I buried my face into my backpack. When I climbed into the car, I ducked down. My adoptive brother sat like a normal person in the backseat, and instead of going in the direction of our house, my adoptive father drove us through a small and complicated neighborhood, there were stop signs every block, and then we came upon an industrial space, then past the industrial space and into what appeared to be a new town. The car stopped. There were small stone and brick buildings situated on a well-manicured hillside lawn like an extremely wealthy person's estate. In the center of the spread was a lake with swans. Someone was feeding them and someone else trimmed the hedges. I thought he was going to drop us off and let us start our lives over in a strange town with a new family, but instead he got out of the car, pulled my adoptive brother out, then dragged him to a small stone building where I saw a door open, and only my adoptive brother went in. Somehow I was spared the experience. I only knew it was a therapist because my adoptive brother told me. He told me that he told the therapist he wanted to be a therapist. Each week was an opportunity for a new lie. The therapist called my adoptive father and told him he couldn't work with a person like that; it was too frustrating.

Think about what therapists have to listen to all day, said my adoptive brother. At least I was saying something interesting.

30

EVERYTHING IN MY memory was significant in relation to his suicide; it was like staring at a wall for hours when you're on drugs, the wall becomes packed with meaning and menace. I stepped outside to mail my rent check. It was a relief to take a break, and I shut the front door with a kick to the brass plate. At the end of the driveway my adoptive parents had installed a whimsical mailbox in the shape of a fat cow, its legs and udders dangled down, forever humiliating my adoptive brother and me. As I shut the mailbox, a police car pulled up. The engine shut off and two policemen got out, I turned away quickly, the car doors slammed shut, and I heard boot heels clicking toward me.

Excuse us, ma'am, do you live here?

I looked at them hesitantly; they looked depressed and impulsive, I wanted to ask them if they ever considered suicide. Because there were two of them, I was very nervous.

I used to live here, I said. Why?

We're just checking in on things, they said. How long have you been here, and how long are you staying?

A couple days. I'm here to offer my support.

That's nice.

I realized one of the police officers was a blonde woman with short hair like a man's, and masculine features, but it didn't make me feel better. She looked meaner than the man.

Are you related to the people that live here? said the woman.

I'm the adoptive sister-daughter.

Are your parents home? We'd like to have a word.

You're welcome to come in, I said, but my adoptive mother isn't feeling well.

So you'll be at the funeral, the female said.

I hope to be.

Give her this, said the man.

It was a small white envelope, *to Mary and Paul.*

I watched the car drive away. I was in another one of my philosophical moods. Ultimately we must take matters into our own hands and decide our own fate, which is what I was beginning to believe my adoptive brother did when he killed himself.

31

THERE WAS A PARK that no one liked near my adoptive parents' house. I liked to go there when I was in high school, because I was always in trouble, and alone, and crying. I hadn't yet come into my Sister Reliability role, I wasn't of service to anyone, not even to myself; I was just another troubled female.

The park was almost always empty. There was a man-made lake with no ripples, some benches scattered around the lake, a tiny wood bridge, a few small man-made hills to run up and down, a grove of elms and oaks. No one went to that park; children hated that park. Perhaps old men who lacked imaginations liked that park. Everyone else thought it was boring, and it was.

It was possibly the worst park in the history of parks. I walked from my adoptive parents' house to that terrible park, and it matched up perfectly with what I pictured, with what I remembered from skipping out of high school to escape to the park, to go and sit underneath a nonnative tree, to smoke a cigarette and smell the fresh-cut grass and geese shit. When I was in high school, they didn't have the funding for the program to remove and exterminate geese. The geese lived their lives, and then some brainless person, I'd guess *a male*, made the decision to collect and exterminate them, because they covered everything in their shit.

My daughter is going to slip and fall, someone said.

She deserves to fall on the shit, I thought, if she can't pay attention to what she's doing. Mankind will go extinct soon. I became interested in that idea. No one was there to stop me, or to say Helen, you are thinking very negative thoughts, humans are not that bad, for example…

The third day of my investigation I sat on a bench in front of the lake devoid of geese. I smoked a cigarette and another. I was *smoking meditatively* when I saw Thomas jogging around, Thomas stretching his legs, Thomas tying his shoes, Thomas putting in his earbuds, Thomas doing jumping jacks, Thomas in a purple polo shirt and black athletic shorts.

Thomas! I called out to him. Thomas!

He ignored me and kept running.

Young lady, said an old man sitting on a bench directly across from me, did you know this park was built on top of an old Indian burial mound?

I was surprised a man even noticed me, I was usually invisible. And most people never registered that I even had a sex, they saw me as a small and shabby adult, someone to be pushed out of the way. I got up from the bench, ignoring the old man, and ran after Thomas. I was very out of shape and by the time I reached him I was gasping and out of breath.

Thomas, I said. I touched his arm.

What more do you want from me? he said as he began to slow his pace. Haven't I told you enough?

Something has been bothering me, I said.

So what's new about that.

I need to know something. Did he ever say anything to you about working with a Korean professor?

He didn't go to college, how could he work with a professor?

He told me he audited the class.

Thomas shook his head and picked up his pace.

Have you ever looked at yourself in the mirror? he said. You constantly have a crazy look on your face. I bet you didn't know that. Well, it's true. I have to go, good luck!

Will I see you at the funeral? I called out, even though I had no idea what time the funeral was.

He kept running farther away. I watched him exit the park, then he made a turn and disappeared past a bus making its own turn. Sweating and exhausted, I threw myself down on a different bench underneath a weeping willow. After I gathered myself, I took out my phone and performed a quick search. There was a Professor Kim who taught at the Marquette law school, with a specialty in criminal law theory and race. My hands trembled as I typed out an email to her. To put it plainly, I informed her of my adoptive brother's suicide. I closed the email by asking her when we might meet for lunch, my treat. The word suicide itself no longer had much meaning; its meaning had been sucked out and now it was simply a husk of a word that I used in relation to my adoptive brother. Utilizing the word suicide in a conversation instead of the phrase *died unexpectedly* emphasized the violence against the self; it cut through the bullshit and brainlessness of talking to strangers about my adoptive brother's death. I pressed send.

Then I paused a moment and responded truthfully to my supervisor's message. I typed that I did not keep good records, but I did remember one day taking my troubled young people to Central Park to play basketball. We borrowed a basketball from someone at the park, and it's possible we lost it. I apologized. Then I apologized for possibly damaging the paper-towel dispensers. I considered calling my supervisor to see how everyone was doing, but I decided it wasn't wise to draw attention to the fact that I was missing work, especially considering I was under an internal investigation. The problem with an investigation is people will continue to investigate until they have found *something*, anything, and only then, when they have found *something*, will they close the investigation. And what would the investigators uncover about me? I wondered. Would they find out that every day was an internal struggle to not destroy the lives of my troubled young people? Would they discover that when I went into my place of employment, unlike all of my coworkers who took the elevator up to the facility, I, as far as I knew, was the only one who walked up ten flights of stairs in order to inhale sharply the aroma of the rubber-encased steps because the smell transported me more lucidly than a dream back to the first grade of Catholic school and how I hid from the nuns in a very similar if not the exact same rubber-encased stairwell simply because I could spend minutes, hours inhaling the delicious fragrant rubber smell? I was very curious about what they would find out about me, in fact one might say I was perversely curious.

32

AS I LEFT THE PARK, I noticed a crowd of people had formed around the bus where Thomas had exited and turned. The bus was still there. An ambulance pulled up and a police car. Then another. The bus driver was talking to the police. People stood around nervously and looked down at something. I saw their mouths open, and their fingers pointing. It appeared the bus had hit a pedestrian.

Instead of investigating the scene, I focused on the status of my own investigation. In order to investigate something, you need to talk to people and you need to get them to say things, helpful things, confessions, etc. I left the park and went in the opposite direction of the bus and the ambulance. I turned onto a busy street, and I walked in the shoulder, right next to cars driving at 50 miles per hour, when some people honked at me and rolled down their windows and screamed at me to get a car. Instead of going home, I headed toward a café.

No one liked to tell me anything, I despaired. Thomas no longer wanted to talk to me. The Moons had nothing to say. Why didn't people like to tell me things? I needed more witnesses and more components. I needed to put his life into an arrangement that made sense. When I arrived at the café, I was dehydrated and exhausted from yelling back at people. It bewildered me, all the people inside the café, sitting and sipping quietly, everyone with a life doing things. The café could move two feet to the left, and everyone would continue their sipping. I ordered a skinny half-caff latte, then took my drink and sat down at a table near the bathroom and began to collect my thoughts. A tall thin woman walked by and then walked back.

Helen? she said. Helen Moran?

Me?

Don't you remember me? She smiled. It's Elena.

I looked at the woman. She seemed familiar, she reminded me of someone from the artistic group, and I shuddered.

I'm not sure who I am to you, I said.

You look exactly the same, she said. I walked by and I said to myself, that's Helen Moran, there she is, after all these years, she's sitting right there in a chair, looking around at things.

Thank you for noticing, I said.

You left Milwaukee, right?

I moved to New York.

It's been a long time since we saw each other, she said. I'm sorry we lost contact.

I never come back here, I said. Not even for holidays.

I'm sorry, she said. Milwaukee has missed you.

I think you've mistaken me for someone else, I said.

Oh, that's not possible, she said. You were unforgettable back then! I'll never forget that performance in the nude with you, Peggy, and Teresa. Or what about that night of absurdist theater? You were in a cardboard boat while two brothers played instruments behind you. You took pictures with a Polaroid camera, then you carelessly threw the pictures into the audience and hit someone in the eye, the picture tore a man's cornea.

I never sat in a cardboard boat, I said. I never tore a man's cornea.

Yes, you did, said Elena. Back then you were an emerging artist and you made assemblages out of boxes, a hundred boxes from a dumpster stacked on top of one another, then someone started that silly rumor, well, I know it's not good to stir up things from the past...

No, I said. Sometimes it's necessary.

She patted my arm.

I won't bother you, of course, but tell me quickly what you're doing back here.

My adoptive brother died, I said, I've come to find out what happened.

Oh dear, she said. Was he ill?

Elena, that is the exact question I asked myself when I heard the news! I said to Uncle Geoff, Was he ill, no one told me he was ill! He wasn't ill, he killed himself, and I'm trying to understand why. There are six possible reasons a person will commit suicide, would you like to know what they are?

I explained to her the six reasons. I told her there were of course more possibilities, including ones I couldn't even begin to imagine. Suicide is everywhere, I went on, impossible to escape from. It must be an attractive solution to the irrational, the depressed, and the pathological.

What do you mean it's everywhere? said Elena.

A few months ago a story circulated around my workplace about a coworker's roommate, a young woman from China who had difficulty speaking English. When she got home one day, she did all of these mundane things, she unpacked the grocery bag, she took out the trash and recycling. She swept the floors. She left the mung beans, a package of glass-thread noodles, and one sweet potato on the counter. Then she went into the bathroom she shared with my coworker. She tied a noose and stepped off the toilet. She hung herself only a few steps away from my coworker's bedroom. Of course she didn't do a very good job, the noose came apart, and she fell down onto the tile, and on the way down, she slammed her head against the toilet. My coworker discovered her on the floor, the noose still partially around her neck, and took her to the hospital. Everyone, according to my coworker, shunned her after she survived her attempt, including my coworker. Who knows why everyone shunned her, except when someone attempts suicide and fails, we feel nothing but ashamed and embarrassed for them.

Better to have succeeded, I said to Elena, better to have died.

Maybe she tried to kill herself because her English was bad, and it was hard to make friends. Who could say? Or what about that French philosopher who threw himself out the window? Perhaps he saw swarms and machinic assemblages everywhere. Who wants to see that? And then there are the people who we always have on suicide alert, the depressed friend or cousin, the ones we always think are about to kill themselves, every time we get a phone call in the middle of the night, we think Dan or Vera finally did it, but we never get that phone call, and those people we thought throughout our entire lives were about to commit suicide end up dying happily of lung disease.

My point is, how is anyone supposed to live with anything? I said to Elena.

33

I WENT OUTSIDE onto the patio, where it was cool in the shade and I could think, as I require a cool temperature in order to think, a cool temperature has always supported not hindered my thinking apparatus. I smoked a cigarette and threw away the box. I do not enjoy how slowly I think and take in information, I thought. How slowly I think and absorb information has always embarrassed me. After a minute or two, I looked up into the café through the glass doors. Elena was still seated at the table where I had sat, and it looked like she was crying.

Talking to her was a distraction, the person I really needed to speak to was dead. I would never talk to him again! I took out my phone and saw there was an entire archive of a conversation with a now-dead person at my disposal. It only now occurred to me that there were clues and traces in the text archive. My adoptive brother was a cryptic person and there were certainly hidden meanings behind each little cloud of gray. UNPACK THE TEXT, I shouted to myself. I began to scroll through our text history and I could say that many of his texts were very basic and practical. KOBE BRYANT!!! said one of them. What was the context? I wondered. I think I thought that the text was meant for someone else, which naturally reminded me of the time he sent me an email from a different name, RICHARDWALSINGHAM@gmail.com. It was in reply to a conversation we were having about what he wanted as a Christmas gift and what to get our adoptive parents, as I usually helped pay for gifts for them, I contributed a very small amount, around ten dollars, even though I had voluntarily removed myself from their lives, I could at least pitch in ten dollars toward their Christmas gifts, which my adoptive brother purchased, most likely with my adoptive father's checks cashed out to himself. And our adoptive family was always very practical about Christmas gifts, people made lists of things they wanted and people bought the things on the lists, and therefore there were no real surprises on Christmas, it was less about gift-giving and more about some kind of exchange, this for that, and although I no longer participated directly in this exchange, my adoptive brother let my adoptive parents know I had contributed toward their gifts, which must have compelled them each Christmas to send me a card informing me that they had donated a small amount of money to the Catholic church in my name, which I never thanked them for or acknowledged because I thought it was an utterly useless, tasteless gift, as

I myself would never personally choose to donate any money to that kind of disgusting pro-child-rape institution. Everyone could have bought themselves the things they wanted and called it a day, I thought. It was strange to receive an email from a Richard Walsingham regarding the purchase of certain gifts for my adoptive parents and my adoptive brother, in fact, I almost deleted the email because I thought it was spam, I only opened it because I had no other new, unread emails in my inbox and I was of course curious about what this Richard Walsingham had to say. When I realized it was my adoptive brother writing from an alias, I immediately asked him who this Richard Walsingham was and why was he pretending to be this person. He never responded to my questions and that email chain was abandoned and we sorted out the Christmas gift situation through text.

A month later, 1/19/13, there was a text of complaint. There was a food bank downtown where once a month our adoptive parents donated several homemade casseroles and hot dishes when it was obvious to anyone that all any homeless person wanted was a slice of pizza or a fucking cheeseburger or a pack of cigarettes, no one wanted their casseroles. He especially hated the smell of the casseroles, the smell of them baking stayed in the air for days, stinking up the entire house, causing him to suffocate in his room.

Part of the purpose of my investigation was to shed some light in the holes and the crevices and the parts of his life that didn't line up, the odd details, etc. It reminded me of shining the flashlight into the crevices of my once-bedbug-infested bed, except instead of bedbugs, I was searching for the odd and the surprising details of someone's life, the strangeness. What was the primary driving force for his life? I wondered. A woman in a green apron came out and swept the patio. Her brisk sweeping movements had a peaceful effect on me and I continued to stare down at the old text conversation that had transformed into an archive of a suicide-ghost.

34

FRIDAY SEPTMBER 27TH: *I'm having a good day, Helen. This weekend I'm going to go on a trip with my mom.* When I received the text, I was inside a bodega in Brooklyn in the early evening. I had just purchased a giant bag of red licorice while my group of troubled people waited outside. A strange feeling overcame me as I read it, because the diction was so odd. And what trip? Where was he traveling to? So much travel in one year, I remembered thinking. I wished I had someone to show the text to, because what he said was so confusing. That night I never followed up or responded, I didn't know how to, and no ethical compulsion came to me, instead I felt strange and colorless, like a piece of wet paper.

He sent it two days before he killed himself.

As I left the bodega, the colorless feeling went away. In front of me was a more immediate situation: I had to get my troubled young people on the A train and somehow conceal the licorice from them. Once on the train, the troubled young people decided to sing loudly and dance in a reckless way, grabbing onto the handlebars and swinging around, kicking their feet up to the ceiling. While most supervisors discouraged this type of disruptive behavior, I did not stop them, just this one time, because I thought it was a good opportunity for them to learn how to keep themselves entertained, and it allowed me to consume the entire bag of licorice unnoticed. By the time I got home, around eight at night, I forgot about the text entirely. I went to bed and slept peacefully and woke up without a care.

Two nights later, the night he killed himself, September 29th, I came down with a case of food poisoning from a bodega bean-and-cheese burrito, I spent the night post-burrito either in the bathroom on the toilet or on the floor, or in bed with the little key in my fist, about to get up to go across the hall to the toilet. It was strange, because my roommate Julie always said I had a cast-iron stomach, I could eat all kinds of disgusting things without consequence, but that night I was sick to my stomach, and for hours everything inside me emptied out.

What had I done? I thought. What had I *not* done? I brought my hands to my face. The woman in the green apron looked up from her sweeping.

I didn't realize anyone was out here, she said. We're closing.

I looked down at my phone; it was later than I thought. I gathered up my things and began to walk back to the house.

I mimicked the woman's sweeping movements to calm myself. It was dark out and the oncoming traffic shone a light on me and I felt singled out, spotlighted for a special purpose.

Why was he so depressed about everything? I said to no one.

At this point in my investigation, I attributed his suicide mostly to depression or perhaps a cry of unhappiness or maybe he simply lost control, even though he never lost control. I decided to take a different route, I crossed the traffic and went past our old Catholic school. I noticed the plastic vestibule had been installed in preparation for winter. This plastic vestibule had a very particular smell, I thought, the smell of the inside of a child's shoes. For a few years I got along very well with the nuns, I saw a little of myself in them, whereas my adoptive brother despised the nuns, he said he would never be able to learn anything from such shriveled-up old prunes. For a moment, I thought about breaking into the school to inhale the aroma of the rubber-encased steps, to see if it was as fragrant as it was over twenty years ago. Then a tear almost came to my eye; I had gone to that school *more than twenty years ago*. Instead of breaking into the school overseen by the nuns and priests, I continued on my way and by the time I got home, I was covered in grass stains and dirt.

I fell into a deep ditch because it was so dark out and I had cut through a forest, not the child molestation forest, a different forest that was unknown to me, and I couldn't see where I was going, and there were trees everywhere and the path was uneven, excuses, excuses, it was so dark! It was some kind of miracle that I had made it home at all. There were holes in the knees of my pants and streaks of oil down the shins. When I fell into the ditch, my knees scraped against some metal scaffolding and construction debris. It dawned on me that someone was trying to build a condo village in the middle of the forest. As I tried to pull myself out of the ditch I must have grabbed onto a piece of twisted metal because there were cuts all over my hands. Some people are lucky, I thought, I have always narrowly escaped total annihilation. I approached the house with my bleeding hands and oil-streaked legs, I saw the house lit up, and from the front lawn, the windows framed the brightly lit wreaths, even my bedroom windows that looked out onto the driveway, the smallest windows of the house, radiated a picturesque cheerfulness, and it wasn't until I took in all of the gladness and cheer that I noticed there were two new cars in the driveway, one with an out-of-state license plate.

35

A FEW MINUTES PASSED as I took a leisurely path around the yard and then entered the house through the garage, which was left wide open, expectantly, and from the garage I went into the laundry room, where I took off my shoes and pants and washed my knees and hands with a bar of white soap. I found some bandages and put them on my cuts. I crept into the hallway, pants-less.

I lurked behind the kitchen door, then I peered around slowly. I saw a family of relatives, and even more shocking was the appearance of the Moon parents plus a young man who I believed was Zachary Moon. Scattered around the kitchen table were a few of my adoptive parents' neighbors, one of them was grinding coffee beans with a whimsical-looking Japanese hand grinder. A woman put a glass pan in the oven and took one out. There were pans with foil on the counter, beverages and trays of cheese and nuts. I hadn't seen any of them in years, relatives or neighbors. They spoke in low and respectful voices. The relatives were on my adoptive mother's side and it gradually became clear to me that they were talking with the neighbors about college applications, the due dates, who was applying where, standardized tests, how expensive everything was, even the applications themselves. All of the neighbors in the kitchen were about to send children off to college, they were good, hearty Catholic breeders. They lived in large, sprawling mini-mansions, which they populated with mini-versions of themselves. Of course the Moons were a little different. Everyone at school thought they were part of a cult.

Zachary was talking to someone, and when he turned around, he caught me watching the scene unfold. He waved and started to approach the door, then I turned away and flew up the stairs, only to run into my adoptive mother. She was coming down the steps with a basket of laundry. I handed her the white envelope from the police. She opened it quickly and seemed upset.

What is it?

A gift certificate to Three Sons, the Greek restaurant.

Why is that upsetting?

What happened to your hands? And where are your pants?

I told her that I fell down into a ditch.

Oh, she said as if it were the most perfectly natural thing in the world for me to tell her that I had fallen into a ditch.

She didn't even ask what kind.

As she passed me she said, the relatives are staying overnight with us. I thought we might put them in your room.

She didn't even give me a chance to say no, no, that is a terrible idea. She was already standing in the foyer talking to a neighbor who occupied her with a very sympathetic look; from the stairs I saw the neighbor's large, wide tearful eyes and nodding head. Whatever the neighbor said moved my adoptive mother to tears, and then the neighbor started crying and it went back and forth and back and forth.

My own eyes did not tear up; I enjoyed my position as the neutral and passive observer. I went into my bedroom, where I noticed the relatives' suitcases and jackets and backpacks had been laid out on my childhood bed. Beneath all of their things was a bedspread I had never seen before. I opened one of the relatives' suitcases. There was a funeral suit neatly folded, a black V-neck sweater, and freshly polished funeral shoes, which made me think of my turtleneck sweater. Where was my turtleneck sweater? On top of the funeral clothing was a giant bottle of Advil.

My own bathrobe and traveler's kit were nowhere to be found. My own canvas suitcase was missing. I opened the closet and found a pair of men's trousers that still had the tags on, possibly a gift for my adoptive brother, but never worn. I put them on, they were a few sizes too large so I found a braided leather belt. There was a pocket in the front, where I deposited my phone. I sat down on my bed for a few moments to collect my thoughts. I noticed that the flowerpots were still covered in white foam, the foam hadn't dissipated and the entire room smelled like an old man's acrid sweat. I had no idea how anyone would be able to fall asleep in my room with that kind of stench, I would sleep happily in the hallway.

I heard the voices of the neighbors and relatives, their voices wafted up from below like a baking smell, and I enjoyed the texture of feeling it gave me. It reminded me of the one and only time my adoptive family hosted a large number of relatives at the house for Christmas when I was in first grade, a happy time, and it was strange to me that the Christmas hosting happened only once since the house was so large and would accommodate comfortably at least ten people at a time. My room seemed to be situated so one could hear everything going on below in the house, and even though the house was so expansive and empty, from the cozy perch of my childhood bedroom, all alone, the house itself felt very small and cheerful. Listening to the voices from below brought me back to that time and how beautiful it was to be alone in first grade, to sit on my bed alone with a book like *The Secret of the Wooden Lady*, and to hear human voices and to know and truly feel that there were people below, and at the same time, to not feel compelled to join them, it was a luxurious feeling to cherish, because the exact texture of that feeling happened so few times in my life. Perhaps it had something to do with being a child and being free but now as an adult I had certain responsibilities to face, like finding out what happened to my adoptive brother, why he killed himself, etc.

With strangers and relatives colonizing the rooms like bacterial pathogens, it would be difficult to continue my investigation, I reflected. Because of their presence, I was forced to be social, I was compelled to be *interactive*. I went back down the stairs and into the laundry room where my adoptive mother was stuffing my childhood bedsheets and comforter and pillowcases into the washing machine.

This house is huge, I said, why don't we put the relatives in one of the guest bedrooms?

Before I was able to warn her about the flowerpot insecticide, she was already saying something.

Those rooms aren't ready, she said sharply. Those rooms haven't been aired out in months. They are not in a suitable condition for guests who have driven all the way from Colorado. It's very simple, Helen. Your father and I know what we're doing. You've never had to host a funeral before. The best thing you can do for us is to calm down, and stay out of the way.

I mopped the foyer and the hallway in the back, I said.

Thank you for that. You're doing your part.

So where did you put my things?

In your brother's room.

The laundry room became small, the ceiling dropped, the walls pressed in. I was sweating. I brought my bandaged hands up to my face in an intense way, designed to get her attention, but she had her back to me. With my bandaged hands, I covered my mouth the way my adoptive brother covered his mouth before he killed himself. I was too stunned to say anything.

Is that okay with you? she said after a minute of silence.

Instead of paying attention to me and my hand-covered mouth, she took a pile out of the dryer, and began to fold someone's underpants neatly and stack them. I felt a blast of heat emanating from the underpants, probably my adoptive father's.

My adoptive brother just died, was on the tip of my tongue, but before I said anything, I heard her say, Helen, you should go say hi to the neighbors and relatives. The relatives are here and they are being very supportive.

And the Moons appeared, I said. Did you invite them?

But she wasn't listening to me; she was carefully measuring out a half-cup of detergent for a new load of laundry.

That brand makes me break out in hives, I said.

It's what we have, she said, I'm doing the best I can, considering the circumstances.

The circumstances, I repeated. Dreadful, wretched circumstances.

It's a difficult time for everyone, she said, but it will all be fine eventually.

Before I said, Yes, but he killed himself, she said, Everything will work out.

She said it less to me, and more as if she were talking to herself. It was then I realized the bandages on my hands were oozing blood.

36

LAST NIGHT I DREAMT I murdered someone. I was a European man. I didn't directly experience killing someone, but I knew it had happened. I was hiding in a room from the police, under a desk, and I knew they were about to arrest me. Jacques, come out, they said. We know you're under the desk. In my dream, I considered killing myself, as a simple way to solve the matter instead of going to jail, but now that he killed himself, I thought in my dream, I wouldn't be able to. Even in my dream, I had an adoptive brother who killed himself. Suicide was off the table for me. I would never be able to commit suicide, because everyone would say that I had copied him.

I went into the first-floor bathroom. There was no mirror, everyone in my adoptive family hated to look in the mirror. Inside the toilet room was a plastic basket with expired medical supplies. I took off my bandages and replaced them. There was blood on my face, I felt its sticky texture on my chin, and I was forced to wash my face, even though I prefer to wash only once a day, if at all. I left the toilet room, and before I reached the staircase, a relative accosted me and drove me into the kitchen, where the neighbors and other relatives were sitting at a table, drinking coffee, admiring the Japanese coffee grinder, and putting foil-covered dishes into the freezer. It was like when my adoptive mother was sick and all the neighbors brought dinner over for a month. When I came into the kitchen, everyone stood up and approached me, even Zachary Moon tried to give me a hug, everyone made sad faces and said how sorry for my loss they were, and they asked what they could do to help, it felt like being swarmed by insects. A grieving assemblage.

At the table not only was there coffee and tea and the grinder but also an uncorked bottle of wine. I was offered a glass by a young man with a red beard, and even though as a general rule I prefer marijuana because I lack an enzyme to properly metabolize alcohol, as I was the center of everyone's attention and care, and the situation was so awkward, as the passive-observer, I accepted the glass, drank it down like water, and accepted immediately a second.

Then the father of the red beard, one of the uncles, stepped out of the swarm and said, Helen, come here.

He pulled me aside and thrust forward his hand.

Uncle Walt, he said.

He said it was strange to be gathered here in suburban Milwaukee and for my adoptive brother not to be present.

It's like he's playing a trick on us, he said, he was a very sly and crafty person. He loved practical jokes. I know I shouldn't have favorite nieces and nephews, but of course he was my favorite. He was everyone's favorite.

All of the relatives and neighbors formed a circle around. They nodded in agreement.

He was my favorite neighbor, said a neighbor, it was always so nice to see him walking the dog. He was so polite. He was friendly, or, well, maybe not exactly friendly, but if you said hi to him, he would say hi back.

And in a very nice way, said the neighbor.

If you needed help with anything, chimed in another, he was there. He was a very reliable and helpful person.

Your brother, said Uncle Walt as he looked at me directly, was a very easy person to get along with. He must have been such a good little brother. It's terrible, what happened to him. If he was experiencing pain or having trouble, he was very skilled at hiding it and covering it up.

My face was flushed; I had no idea what Uncle Walt was saying or from where he received his information.

Did my adoptive father tell you that? I said. Did he tell you that he was hiding things from them?

Oh no, he said, it's just something I'm hypothesizing, based on the last time we saw him. You see, Helen, a few months ago he came out to visit us in Colorado, which was very unexpected. I think he reached out to us through your mom. He had an interest in fly-fishing, so we, my son and I, took him fly-fishing. I showed him how to tie lures, we went to the sporting-goods store and bought him some boots and a vest and a hat. We outfitted him expertly. He told us that he had always been interested in fly-fishing, in fact I remember he said that he thought it seemed like a very meditative thing to do, that was exactly what he said, he was such a perceptive person. He's right, it is a very meditative and calming activity. We had a really good day fly-fishing.

Tears came to his eyes.

So naturally, he said, we were very sad when we heard the news.

Did fucking Uncle Geoff call you? I said.

No one heard me.

Does anyone know Uncle Geoff? I said.

Is he on your dad's side? said the young man with a red beard. The red beard stood behind Uncle Walt, who was seated at the table, and it looked like he might cry, too.

Jonathan has never lost anyone close, said Uncle Walt, until now.

It astonished me that my adoptive brother had flown out to Colorado to go fly-fishing, which he never told me about, he never even told me he had an interest in fly-fishing. Where did that come from? I wondered. It was very strange, the image of him standing in a stream waving around a bamboo rod puzzled me and seemed at odds with who I thought he was. I pictured my adoptive brother, the fly-fisherman, in rubber boots and canvas clothing, like a character out of *A River Runs Through It,* a pointless book I was forced to read in high school for no particular reason whatsoever, except that there was a film tied to it, and then I was forced to watch the film. It was an image, the fly-fisherman, impossible to reconcile with what I knew about him. The more I tried to picture it, the more I started laughing! People shifted in their chairs and looked at me uncomfortably.

He was certainly a special person, said a neighbor.

I listened to a few more reminisces of my adoptive brother's virtuous nature and wonderful personality, and it became clear to me that the entire conversation would be focused entirely on him for the next hour or so.

So he became a fly-fisherman, I said to myself, and what am I supposed to do with that information?

No one asked me how I was doing or what I had been up to.

No one said, *Helen, it's been a long time since we've seen you, what have you been doing with your life?*

No one said, Helen, what's it like living in New York City? No one even asked me if I had a boyfriend! Perhaps they thought I was too ugly to attract a man. Little did they know, in my experience, even the most repulsive women will attract *someone*!

The entire situation irritated me and I also knew if my adoptive brother were alive, he would hate it, he would hate all of these people talking about him behind his back. I decided to leave, and headed toward the toilet again. Zachary Moon followed behind me. I said hello, and tried to keep myself from vomiting.

Is it okay if I go first? I said.

I was looking for you, he said.

He pulled me into the second living room, where it was empty. When he pulled my arm, I tumbled to the floor and almost threw up on the carpet in front of the piano.

Helen, he said as he helped me up, don't you think it's strange that his suicide seemed to come out of nowhere? How well do you think you knew your brother?

I burped, some vomit rose up in my throat, and I employed the Swiss mountain stream technique to swallow it down. Then I told him about the time my adoptive brother visited me in New York, about the status of my investigation, and I went over the six reasons people commit suicide.

He looked at me with a strange and intense emotion, it seemed like he wanted to shake me, or to kiss me. I swerved my head away, in case. He pretended he didn't notice anything, and told me that the article I cited missed a reason, the reason he believed my adoptive brother killed himself: a *philosophical reason*, but I didn't get to hear his explanation; I had to pull myself away from him, so I would be able to throw up alone, comfortably and quietly.

37

WHEN I WAS A FRESHMAN in high school, everyone called me *spinster from a book*, because of how ugly I was, and the state of my generic, off-brand clothing and shoes. At that time I had not discovered clothes from the dumpster. I wore beige caftans from Kmart in the summer, and during the school year, a beige shirt and pants uniform. From far away, it probably looked like I was nude. If I walked past a boy in the hallway, he shrieked and made screeching sounds. IT'S THE SPINSTER FROM A BOOK! Then he would stick his finger in his mouth. The truth was, I didn't mind the quaint and old-fashioned insult; I thought spinsters were interesting because of the books I read,

Jane Austen and George Eliot. Of course, even in their novels, the spinsters were married off eventually. Perhaps the book that left the greatest impression on me from that time was Kafka's diaries, I admired his entries of despair and complaint, I tried to absorb them as a way to perceive and understand the world because I too had despair and complaints. And I'll never forget
8 how he ended them: *You too have weapons*. END.

Who, exactly, has weapons? Did he mean me? My adoptive brother?

At the age of sixteen, I was obsessed with a person I didn't know, and I used this obsession to get out of the house and see the world outside of suburban Milwaukee. I followed Fiona Apple around on tour across the country one summer by myself, I bought bus and plane tickets, after saving up every paycheck from a seasonal mall job at the incense store. Instead of staying at motels, I tried to befriend innocent-looking people at the shows and hint that I needed a place to spend the night, it worked mostly with young unattractive men who were alone, young men with canes, etc. The other nights I spent in hostels or even in 24-hour diners, I went to as many shows as possible, I would arrive early, and perch myself by the backstage door, usually with a pathetic stuffed animal, and I can only imagine the intense pity she must have felt for me as she came upon me standing by myself with a stuffed animal, waiting by the door like some poor orphan out of Dickens, it probably ruined her day. One time I gave her a notebook with poetry, not my poetry, of course, but poetry by Sylvia Plath, I tore out my favorite poems and glued them into the notebook, I myself didn't write poetry, I had no interest in writing anything, I thought poetry was boring but cool, and she asked me why I liked Sylvia Plath, she seemed genuinely interested to know why, and I told her I liked the poem about shoes that rhymed, and Fiona Apple sort of smiled, she told me to read Maya Angelou's *I Know Why the Caged Bird Sings*, then her tour manager pulled her away from me, wait, she's trying to tell me something, no wait, but she was easy to pull away because she was small, meanwhile the security guards were assholes, and they made fun of me, some of them called me chink, but I didn't care, my heart lifted when she came out onstage to perform, because she waved the stuffed animal around and put it on top of her piano, where it remained until the end of the show, and when she left the stage, she took it with her. What did she do with all of them? I wondered. She probably has a room in her house filled with stuffed animals from starving once-orphans like myself, I thought, or maybe she donated them to a children's hospital or a preschool in need.

As I remember that time and how colorless everything was, everything except Fiona Apple, I realize it's possible I was as miserable as my adoptive brother, and I understood how this misery and depression would lead to suicide. Until I returned home, I forgot that for a brief moment, I myself considered suicide, I thought about cutting my wrists with plastic razors when I was in high school, and I considered it again before I escaped Milwaukee. My adoptive mother was correct, *I was very dramatic*. But I didn't kill myself for some reason or another. Inside me was a force that wanted to stay alive.

38

LIKE MOST NORMAL PEOPLE, my life force ebbed and flowed, ebbed and flowed. At times I felt euphoric for no reason, perhaps a troubled person gave me a high five and told me I was cool, and then, an hour later, I started to feel depressed, like nothing was worth it, everything I did was a waste. I was currently on the tile floor of the upstairs bathroom, a bathroom connected to my adoptive brother's bedroom in a house full of relatives and neighbors, where I was resting after an hour spent violently throwing up and retching and then forcing myself to gag by sticking a finger down my throat in a desperate attempt to end the spell of nausea that had seized my body.

We can get sidetracked, I said to no one, and off the track completely, if we only pay attention to certain things, the same things over and over. If we don't widen our scope and look at the broader picture, we may find ourselves repeating and looping endlessly, pointlessly. You have to continually see the world in new ways or else you get stuck, I said to no one. So perhaps one day, when you wake up, you pretend to be Fiona Apple, imagine what your daily life would be like.

It was a unique perspective, on the floor, and I began to notice pieces of dried-up mucous stuck to the wall along the baseboards, crusty pieces of snot attached to the wall. It was my adoptive brother's mucous; no one else in the house used this bathroom, as it was attached to his bedroom. Perhaps this was part of the cruel plan Chad Lambo talked about. He left the snot for us to discover and bring back to life. When I tried to peel it off, it broke into pieces, sharp pieces of dried-up mucous cut through the bandages and sliced into my fingers and made them bleed all over again. Some of the wallpaper ripped off.

I stood up, went to the sink, washed the blood off my hands, splashed my face with water and rinsed out my mouth, and replaced my bandages. When I was little, I used to say bad things and tell lies, like all little children. Especially when I lied, my adoptive mother picked me up and carried me to the sink and rubbed my mouth with a bar of white soap, probably Dove. There was always a bar of white soap by the sink. I wondered what the soap would taste like now. As a thirty-two-year-old woman, I picked up the soap, which had bubbles on top from my previous washing, and I placed a bit of the end inside my mouth. I gagged immediately, it was disgusting, more disgusting than the taste of sperm. I'd rather swallow sperm, I said to no one, I'd rather eat a tray of pubic hair. My adoptive mother's punishment came back to me clearly and I pictured how frenzied she became as she wiped the bar of soap all over my mouth, and I saw her throwing down the bar of soap in disgust and dropping me to the floor. I was seven years old. It actually made me feel a little better to gag again, to get the alcohol out of my body.

A person knocked at the door.

Is someone in there? a relative asked.

Yes, Helen's in here, I said. To be honest, I'm not doing well.

Should I get your father?

Please don't do that, anything but that!

The relative didn't hear me, because after a minute of silence, my adoptive father knocked at the door.

Helen, what's going on in there? Other people need to use the bathroom. You can't just stay in there all night. Don't be so selfish.

I know there are other people out there and it's very selfish of me to hog the bathroom, I said, but there are other bathrooms. Can't they use those?

Your aunt's pill container is in that bathroom, and her things, he said. Open the door.

I pictured the other people in the hallway. They hovered around the door and waited anxiously. I picked up a towel from the closet, maybe the same one I had masturbated with, and wrapped it around my head. I opened the door and, without a word, stepped out.

My face was covered with the towel, but I knew if I walked approximately twenty steps and turned to the left, I would come to the door of a never-used guest room that functioned mostly as storage for my adoptive father's hoarding tendencies. No one even tried to stop me.

It's all yours, I heard my adoptive father say to a relative.

The bathroom door shut.

39

TWO STEPS FORWARD, ONE step back. One step forward, two back. I was very far away from where my adoptive parents wanted to put me: my adoptive brother's bedroom. Thirty steps, fifty steps away, who could say? I was in a room that no one paid attention to. It was drab and filthy. A pullout couch covered in cigarette burns took up most of the room. No one in the house smoked, the smoker must have been the previous owner, the couch must have been owned by someone else and purchased from Goodwill. The rest of the room had been taken over by stacks of books, papers, files, documents. The room was nothing more than a paper landscape, with one single window that looked out onto nothing, the panes of glass covered in thousands of fly carcasses and spiderwebs, impossible to see out of. I sat on the couch. I felt like I was sitting in the most depressing and disgusting waiting room, worse than the Milwaukee DMV. The room always smelled like body odor, even though no one ever spent any time in it unless one was forced to. Sometimes, when we were little, my adoptive father locked us up in this room. It was a real and serious punishment worse than being spanked. Go to the smelly room, he would say, and think about what you did. To get out, we would have to beg. To be put in a begging position as a child sickened me even more than the bar of soap in my mouth.

For the first time in my life, I realized I disagreed with Kafka. My adoptive brother and I had no weapons, not even metaphorical ones. We were too dumb to figure out how to climb out of the window and onto the roof to escape. We were too dumb to do anything except beg.

I looked down at my phone. There was a text from Steve. How are you doing? he wrote. My roommate Julie must have told him what happened. FINALLY, someone asked me how I was doing! I almost burst into tears. The kindness, the humanity of the question shocked me. No one had ever asked me that before. Or at least it had been a long time. I didn't write anything back to Steve, I thought it would be more mysterious that way, he would be forced to interpret my silence. When I looked up, I noticed the paper landscape was covered in a fine film of dust, and I was compelled to use my masturbation towel as a duster. As I went about the room and began to wipe things down, I started to feel sick. I could hardly breathe, all of the fucking dust molecules flew into my lungs, poisoning me, making me feel nauseated all over again.

I fled from the junk room, coughing, and into my adoptive parents' suite, and once inside the bathroom, I helped myself to a tiny cup of water. Next to the bathroom was a door to a gigantic walk-in closet, which they shared. I opened it and went in. I walked along my adoptive mother's side. It was the size of my side of the shared studio apartment. Her clothes, most of them plain, a few colorful and cheerful blouses, took up an entire side. There was a shelf near the floor with a jewelry box, empty, and above it, a faded, tattered copy of the French Impressionist painting SUNLIGHT STREAMING THROUGH PINK FLOWERS. I touched the paper lightly, and that light touch caused it to rip off the tack, then it fluttered to the floor, where I left it.

My things were in my adoptive brother's bedroom, I remembered. It's simple; just go in there, I thought, go into there and get your things. I went out into the hallway and marched up to the door. I pictured myself opening the door, and then what would happen? I would turn into dust; I would see all of my enemies; I would walk into a white oblivion.

The strip of light was gone; someone must have turned off the light. What if that person was still in there? I wondered. I put my ear to the door: silence. Was it a mistake to go into his bedroom? Mistakes have been made before. I have made plenty of them. Was it too soon after the death? No one was around me to ask. Everyone had gone to bed early; everyone had set their alarms for 6 a.m. I had heard them talking about the funeral in the kitchen, it was scheduled for tomorrow morning, even though no one directly asked me to go, not even my adoptive parents. I'll show them. I'll just show up and sit in the front row of the church, right in front of Chad Lambo, and everyone will see me and my sisterly mourning, I will create a mourning spectacle of myself.

I opened his bedroom door. With the hallway light on, I saw a small desk light, I went in, turned it on, and closed the door. I looked around the room, which was sparsely furnished, even sparser than my own. Then I turned on the ceiling light. There were no knickknacks, one shelf, one desk and metal chair, one twin bed with a metal frame. I recognized on the shelf a book I purchased during a period of teenage decadence, *How To Stop Time*, a memoir about an elegant and sophisticated female heroin user who kept her heroin in glassine envelopes. The image of the glassine envelopes stayed with me for almost sixteen years. He snuck into my room and stole things, I said to no one. He took my things. I sat down on the bed and I ran my hand across the bedspread, then I stood up and lifted it off. Because of my fear of bedbugs, I knew exactly how to examine a bed. I ripped off the top sheet, then the fitted sheet. With all my strength, I lifted up the mattress. What was I looking for? I wondered. Everything was freshly laundered; the sheets were sparkling white with a faint bleach smell, the mattress spotless. I inspected the pillowcases: no traces of blood or drool or bedbug feces.

It wasn't physically clear a human had ever occupied this room. The desk was situated in front of a large window. It was too dark to see out, but I knew there was a large tree outside, the tree that depressed him. A large houseplant was placed upon the desk, blocking the view of the tree. Instead of looking at the depressing tree, he must have looked at this depressing plant.

I went over to the closet and opened it; I braced myself for a tremendous odor. Of course, I had spent a lot of time imagining what was inside it, days and days of visualizing that landscape, and when the material reality did not match up, I was, for a second, astonished. Someone, most likely my adoptive mother, had cleaned it out and remodeled it. To clarify, my adoptive mother *paid* someone to clean and remodel it. She paid someone, a professional closet designer, to rip out the rotting wood with the dead animal and replace it with shiny and smooth pieces of plywood, to build in drawers and shelves, to add an adjustable rod with cedar block hangers and assorted places for shoes and hats and ties. A ceiling light switched on automatically when the door opened. There was a floor-length mirror that reflected back the bed. I saw I had a puzzled expression on my face, which became even more puzzled when I realized there was one item of clothing in the entire wardrobe. My puzzlement turned to joy when I realized it was my black ribbed turtleneck. My black ribbed turtleneck! I took off my shirt, and slipped the turtleneck over my head, and I saw in the mirror it was a perfect fit. I decided I would sleep in it, which would cut down on the time it would take to get ready in the morning. My adoptive mother must have put it in the closet, along with my suitcase and traveler's kit, which were on the closet floor. I took a pill to calm myself, to make the information I took in rational. All of my things were lit up in a yellowish light. It was nothing short of a great pleasure to be reunited with my objects, and there was true comfort in them. But there was nothing of his. He left behind almost nothing, not even a pair of socks. It occurred to me how quiet it was in the room. The silence shocked me, causing a sharp pain to needle up and down my legs, which forced me to sit down at his desk. I realized I had not paid enough attention to what was on the desk.

Someone had turned off the desk fan, the ever-persistent desk fan that provided background noise and peace, his lifelong companion. The fan had been unplugged and someone had wrapped the cord neatly around the neck. As I sat at the desk, I observed that the room did not appear to be a crime scene. I did not see any blood or brain matter. I did not see a body. There was a cleaning-product aroma.

You must air out this disgusting house! I said to no one. His laptop computer, a basic PC, was on the desk. I turned it on and when I looked up, I saw the balding European man. He was holding a cup of coffee. I noticed his shoes were loafers open at the toe. He took a sip and nodded at me. Then he opened the door and strode out. I got up to close the door, and I looked both ways in the hallway. I went back to the desk and examined the computer. I clicked all over the place. The contents of the hard drive had been emptied, and erased. The background was the computer's default wallpaper. It chilled me to the bone. This suicide was not an impulsive act of desperation; it had been thought out and planned well in advance. Now the only question was how long ago, how long ago did the thought he could kill himself pass through his brain? I didn't even have a potential motive, except the six reasons, plus one philosophical reason that I didn't even know. I stared for an eternity at the blue patterned wallpaper. Then I clicked on the trash icon. The entire hard drive was erased, except one document.

A NOTE ABOUT SWANS AND ORGANS

—

SEPTEMBER 2013

I AM X. MORAN, born February 10 1984.

Who am I to you?
I'm a person, a Korean adoptee.
I have two parents and one sister.
I have a mom in Korea.

What am I to you?
Inside me are organs that keep me alive.

* * *

This past year so much has happened to me.

I am about to drive to the hospital. So much happened. Here are the highlights from the past year.

I hope you understand.

2013

Jan.—Nothing

Feb.—I was up late one night, and I clicked on this link to a program about a young woman who was about to die, because she was waiting for an organ. She was so far down on the list, she probably died after the program. This was the first time I had heard of something like that happening and it made me upset. Why should people die like that, when there are so many healthy people with extra organs they don't need? It didn't seem fair.

Mar.—I had my first living organ donation interview. The nurse made me give two references. I put down Helen, and Zach. My hope is that they don't call Helen, I can't think about what she would tell them. They asked me a lot of questions and did all these tests. In case this one doesn't work, I made appointments in St. Louis, Janesville, Chicago.

Maybe the best thing about this month was an orphanage called me. I couldn't really understand the woman, she had a bad accent, but she told me my mom in Korea was looking for me! After all the time I spent looking for her! It made me really happy. She gave me more information, and a contact number for a translator.

Apr.—I received my first letter from my mom translated into English! It was cool. She asked me how I was doing and she said she felt guilty about giving me up. She said it wasn't her idea. She asked me to come to Korea to meet her. I didn't tell anyone. I wanted to tell Helen since she was the one who told me to stop searching. But that would have been like saying I told you so. No one likes it when people do that.

Also I was rejected as a living donor on grounds that I didn't understand what I was doing. The doctor felt I was too young. I'm almost thirty! I went to the interview in St. Louis. I was rejected from Chicago. It's terrible to receive these rejections, it feels bad. They told me to apply again in five years. What am I doing wrong?

May—I went to see a kidney doctor right here in Milwaukee, Dr. Abe. I used dad's insurance card, which was a mistake because the bill was sent to our house. My parents don't know anything about what I'm doing. I'm positive they wouldn't understand. I tried to intercept the bill, I checked the mail every day, but I must have missed it. Or it was never sent.

I wrote my mom and I sent it to the translator. We have made plans to meet in Seoul! It's crazy, but she really wants to meet me. I imagine her as a short Asian woman with a round face. She says she washes dishes at a restaurant, and she lives above it. It made me feel bad. But I guess it could be worse.

Jun.—I have never liked traveling but I have decided I will travel this year, I will learn how to do it for a greater cause. I flew to

Colorado and stayed with relatives. I told them I was interested in fly fishing. They dressed me up in fly fishing gear and we went out to a mountain stream. The water was cold. We caught so much fish we didn't know what to do with it. I wanted to throw it back. I have always hated the taste of fish. We kept eating fresh fish every night for dinner. I put it into my mouth then spit it into a napkin. The truth was there was a doctor I wanted to see, and I had an interview with him. I have never cared about fly fishing.

Jul.—Before I left, I got another rejection.

I went to see Helen in July, where she very kindly put me up in her TINY apartment in NYC. What stood out to me was going to the zoo with her, and a collection of the saddest most pathetic animals I have ever seen. They looked like a crazy person's household pets. I stayed with her for one night and from there, I booked a one-way flight from JFK to Seoul, to finally meet my mom!

Aug.—Time's going to slow down this month because I have a lot to say.

I had never been so nervous or excited. I still didn't tell anyone, not even my parents, especially not them, because I wasn't sure it was real. It felt like good luck and I didn't want to ruin it. I wasn't even sure it was real until the airplane landed at the Korean airport, where a translator met me, and took me to the orphanage. I was placed there two months after I was born, almost thirty years ago. I didn't even tell Helen, although the orphanage asked me for an emergency contact and I gave them what I thought was her phone number, but I might have just made something up. I think Helen might be an undiagnosed bipolar or schizophrenic, but she's figured out a way to live with it, although I will say she was kind of dressed like a homeless person and I can't believe she takes care of people as her job (!). I don't trust therapists or psychiatrists anyway.

I was so excited to meet my mom, but also terrified. I wondered if we would look alike and I knew we wouldn't be able to understand one another, still, I just thought it would be cool to meet her, and to say hello (!) after all these years. The translator helped me make an appointment to meet my mom the following day, after I got over the jet lag and stuff. That night I went to a hostel and I couldn't fall asleep. I left and ended up at a 24 hour café. I bought a bottled water and one cup of rice, and read a book, *Blood Meridian*, which is about this monstrous human being named The Judge and in the end he rapes the other main character in the bathroom? It makes me upset and I never understand it. I've reread it like ten times and I'm still not sure about the ending. I was up all night at the café and into the next day when finally someone asked me to give up my seat, because the café was so busy. Actually, I have no idea if that's what the guy said because he was speaking Korean, but he kept making this go away gesture at me, and then he pointed to the door.

So I went to the hostel to change my clothes. And something happened to me. I looked in the bathroom mirror. There were other people washing up, too, but eventually they left, and I was still there. I looked at myself, and became confused. I didn't know who I was or what I was doing in Korea. It didn't make sense. It was like a double consciousness sort of thing and it was scary. Everything in my life split along a line. And now comes the part you probably won't believe, but... I didn't go to the meeting. I was really freaked out, I felt like if I met her, I would see this other life I might have had, and it would be impossible to have it make sense with the life I did end up leading, the one with mom and dad and Helen.

So... it's true. I didn't go to the appointment to meet my biological mom. I couldn't do it. It now reminds me of this thing my mom in Milwaukee told me. When I was little, they had books about adoption for us. I never wanted to read them. Helen read them, she loved all those books, she told my parents she loved reading about herself, but I told my mom I thought there was something bad in them. It's true. Don't open doors that should remain closed. It sounds stupid, but in my life, it's true.

Let me tell you a couple more things about Korea. Sometime after I skipped meeting my biological mom, I walked to a park, where I saw an old man feeding a family of swans. He was standing on a rowboat in the middle of an artificial lake in the middle of the city. Something about the way he interacted with the swans told me that he had been their lifelong caretaker. But then something bad happened. Some of the more aggressive, dominant swans began to peck at him. And the next thing I knew, he lost his balance, he was knocked off the little boat. There were splashes in the water, and I saw swan wings flapping violently, blocking the old man from getting to the lake's surface. The sound they made was so loud. The man drowned. The entire time, I thought I could yell for help, but it happened so quickly, in a matter of minutes, I just didn't do anything but watch what happened. Eventually, some other people showed up and started screaming at me in Korean. The police came and fished out the body. I sort of shrank away from the scene and went back to the hostel.

I had ten messages waiting from the translator at the orphanage. As soon as I was back inside my cramped airless room, someone knocked at the door. I didn't move to answer it. When the person went away, I used the hostel's computer to book my ticket back to the United States. The computer was chained to the desk, an old desktop model.

Sep.—I have always been kind of a failure at everything. I can say with confidence that I was good at one thing: I could memorize long passages from books and if you asked me what page it was on, I would be able to tell you. But what kind of job can you get with that skill? It's pretty useless.

I think Helen used to get freaked out that I memorized an entire book on trees.

But what's not to like about trees?

I used to possess more things, but over the past few years, I've started to give everything away. Someone else out there could put it to use better than me.

That's how I feel about my organs and my body. Someone else could put it all to better use than me, someone in need, someone who wants to stay alive.

A week ago, I fell, and my face hit the floor. I tried to kill myself with pills, the easy way out. It was a moment of weakness and it almost destroyed my entire plan. I was really pissed off at myself. My nose didn't break, but my front teeth fell out, it was pretty humiliating. I'm so ashamed of that. But it taught me something about suicide. That you have to follow through with the plan.

The dentist was going to fit me in for an emergency appointment, but in the end I didn't go. I didn't think my teeth mattered.

I've always wanted to do good things for other people, but I never did them for myself.

A couple weeks ago I acquired the gun. I thought I could do it with pills, but that was selfish. I will take my gun with me,

I will drive to the hospital and sit in my car right outside the emergency room door. I will call the police and 911. I will leave detailed instructions about what my body and organs are to be used for. I will shoot myself carefully in the head, but not so my skull blows up. If I do it correctly, I will not feel anything. The car can be sold to help cover the costs of my funeral.

My organs and skin and eyes and tissues are to be donated to those who are about to die, every person that is last on any organ donation list, all of my physical material is to go to them.

This is my way of doing something right in the world.

I hope you understand what I have decided.

I've wanted to die since I was eighteen. I kept myself alive for as long as I could. This is the moral answer to that feeling.

When I was little I used to go swimming and I thought I could die by holding my breath. Every time I almost did it, I got scared.

When I was little I lied a lot. Helen and I played confession and I fell in love with lying. Our mom washed our mouths with soap, and after a while, I started to like the taste of it. Or maybe I'm tricking myself. I guess I got used to it.

I'm not scared anymore. You can't do it and be scared.

Personally, I think my life was beautiful. No one else would think it's beautiful, but it was enough for me.

You have to believe in what you're doing.

I hope you understand what I have done.

It's possible I have lied about a lot of things, but everything I have said here is entirely true.

I hope you understand.

THE LAST DAY

40

WHEN MY ADOPTIVE BROTHER died, he didn't leave anything for me, not even a letter addressed directly to me, just a document for anyone to read, and addressed to whom? No one in particular. What he left was for the people in need, the people who needed actual help, troubled people with failed organs and missing eyes and ears and tissues, *I want to give it all away.*

The morning of the funeral, I kept rereading his document, and I was astonished that my adoptive brother thought I might be bipolar or schizophrenic. I kept reading that part about myself, over and over, I ran my finger across the computer screen, and

I touched the word *schizophrenic*. The oil from my finger caused the word to shimmer psychedelically. I kept searching for the parts where he wrote my name, *Helen*. I touched my name and made it shimmer. It was so reassuring to read Helen this or Helen that. I exist. In someone else's world, I exist. I wanted to run around in a park or on a hilltop and shout to people, I was in his life! I played a major role, fuckers!

I would have to show it to my adoptive parents, or perhaps they had already read it, there was no way to know, but at the funeral I would ask them. At the funeral, I told myself, would be the appropriate place to ask. One step forward. Two back. One back. Two forward. A few minutes after reading his document for the tenth time, I was proved wrong when I said he didn't leave me anything. He left behind my pamphlet, and when I opened one of the brand-new closet's drawers, there was something in shrink-wrap. I picked it up and examined it. *Bitches Brew* by Miles Davis in vinyl form. I knew he had left it for me, and me alone. Tears came to my eyes. At six in the morning, I heard doors open and close, people padding into the bathroom. I heard people talking. I heard someone get sick in the bathroom.

I checked my email and read a message from my supervisor, he said he wanted to talk to me on the phone and he would call later today, that hopefully I would be around. Perhaps more importantly there was an email from Professor Kim. She wrote to say how sorry she was for my loss, but she had never met my adoptive brother. She had three assistants, one for research and the others for teaching, and they were all female. She didn't have any auditors this semester, and she had never heard his name before. She closed by asking if there was anything else she could do.

For a long time, I looked out the window at the depressing tree. I had moved the plant and desk fan to the floor. The few things he had left behind, I arranged simply, perhaps my greatest talent. Then I began to sob again. The hysterical sobbing person returned and when I looked in his closet mirror, I didn't recognize myself. An ugly vein the size of a child's thumb burst in the middle of my forehead, so it looked like there was a wrinkled worm underneath my skin. As I stared at myself in his closet mirror, I remembered two stories I heard my adoptive mother tell Chad Lambo in the living room the first real day of my investigation. At the time I couldn't process them, but now they made sense, and the stories animated the person everyone thought he was and wasn't, the stories brought him back to life. I liked stories like that, stories that would make me feel as if I understood something about him. When I think of them, I thought, I see a ghost and the traces left all over a person's life.

It was the summer of college graduation for my adoptive brother's friends, and everyone came home to relax and see their families before starting new lives. Everyone met up at a bar in our neighborhood, an American Legion hall-like place. Almost everyone from his favorite time in Catholic elementary school was there. When I think about his life, I'm sure that third grade was his best time, the time he could be who he was and exist comfortably. That night, in his early twenties, his friends drank the tavern's entire supply of beer. And he paid for everyone's drinks that night, everyone in the bar, even strangers who happened to stop in for a drink. The bartenders worked very hard, it was said, and besides paying for everyone's drinks, he left everyone who worked that night an enormous tip.

The second story was more recent. A week before he ended his life he told my adoptive mother that he was going to a ball. For once, she didn't have to ask him a lot of questions, he simply went into great detail about what it would be like. He said the women would wear gowns and gloves, the men would be in tails and top hats. Ice sculptures were set out. Someone dropped off a few swans that would parade around. An octet would play, then a jazz band and maybe even a swing band to cap off the night. Everyone would dance. He would find the ugliest girl who appeared to be alone, and ask her to dance. After he asked her, in a certain light, she would become very beautiful. They would waltz. He described platters of shrimp cocktail set on ice trays, roasted duck with orange sauce, and a chocolate fountain. He would eat white rice. There would be vats of white rice cooked and warmed exactly the way he liked it. Men would play croquet on the lawn, women would whisper in clusters in the bathroom. He told her he rented a tuxedo for the occasion. He said he went to the mall and bought black dress shoes and shoe polish. My adoptive mother told him how happy she was for him. She was overjoyed. When she asked him when the ball was, he said the evening of September 29th, the night he killed himself.

41

AT SEVEN IN THE MORNING, someone knocked emphatically on the door, which frightened me; I felt how wide my eyes were opened. I was sitting up in the bed, already dressed. I decided I would attempt to play the good adoptive daughter, I would go along with whatever my adoptive parents said, even if Chad Lambo asked me to do something, I would do it without complaint or questioning or criticism. I would shut my mouth.

Helen, said my adoptive father through the door, I need you to do something for us.

What's that? I said.

I almost said, Sister Reliability, here to help.

We need you to take your brother's car and go pick up a package from the photography department at the drugstore near the café.

Why can't I take your car? I said. Then I remembered, no questions or complaints!

Can I come in for a second?

Before I answered, he opened the door, came in, and sat down at the desk. I noticed he was fully dressed in funeral garb, a white dress shirt, black pants, black shoes. I smelled shoe polish, most likely applied late last night.

How are you this morning? he asked.

Instead of exchanging pleasantries, I gestured toward the computer, then asked him if he had looked at the document. My adoptive father's face became very sad.

We read it a couple days ago, he said. We had no idea how sick he was.

What do you mean by sick?

Mentally ill.

Why wasn't he seeing a therapist then? Did you know he wanted to die?

My adoptive father began to shake; he was shaking and then he bowed his head down. Tears rolled off his face into his shirt and before long, his white dress shirt was soaked with dark circles and patches like lakes and ponds. I was stunned. There was silence, he always spoke at a delay, outside of time, until he looked up, and his eyes looked directly into mine.

I keep going back to a week ago, he said. We went to a Greek restaurant. It was his favorite restaurant, not only because they had everything you could imagine on the menu, not only because the servers remembered his order perfectly, but because they served plain steamed white rice and unseasoned roasted white chicken especially well. In fact that very meal happened to be their house specialty, that was the meal they were famous for. It was my favorite restaurant, too, I loved their beef vegetable soup and homemade crackers. Helen, do you think I'll ever be able to go there and eat their beef vegetable soup without getting sick to my stomach?

A couple days ago, I accidentally drove by the Greek restaurant. It was a mistake; I had forgotten what I was doing, where I was going, I was in a complete fog. In hindsight, I probably shouldn't have been driving, but I was supposed to meet Father Luke and Chad and your mother and instead of meeting Father Luke and Chad and your mother, I was driving nowhere and I had to turn around and I went right past the Greek restaurant where your brother and I had a final meal together. Of course I had no idea it would be our final meal; if I had known it was to be our final meal I would have insisted we go somewhere else, I would have insisted we go to an expensive restaurant as far away as possible, somewhere outside the city limits, a restaurant I wouldn't care if I ever returned to. I would have insisted we go to a place like that. Because when I drove by the Greek restaurant a couple days ago, I had barely digested the fact that your brother was dead. It hadn't sunk in even though sometime around three in the morning of September 30th, I saw his body in the emergency room hospital bed hooked up to multiple machines, and even though I was the one who made the decision, even though I was the one who told the doctors not to resuscitate, it had not fully sunk in that he was gone, that there was no longer a person there, my son whom I loved and cherished, my favorite person in the world. I knew that to resuscitate him would be to impose upon him a life of utter embarrassment and humiliation. To fail at suicide would have been a catastrophe. For him, to live a life as a suicide survivor would be something far greater than death, do you understand? So you could say your mother and I did what was right for him and by him. In fact, I'll say we did *the just thing*, and we told the doctor not to resuscitate, we repeated it twice at 4 a.m. in the morning of September 30th at the hospital closest to our suburb. And yet when I passed the Greek restaurant a couple days ago, I pulled over immediately. It's on a very busy street, you know where it is, Helen, it's nearly always impossible to find parking, it's on the most traffic-congested street in the city. And as I pulled over into the right shoulder, in front of the Greek restaurant, cars blasted their horns at me, they swerved away angrily, rightfully so you could even say, and I got out of the car and was sick to my stomach. I emptied the contents of my stomach, and the cars continued blasting their horns at me. Some people yelled at me, Motherfucker! Get out of the way! The owner of the Greek restaurant came out to see what was going on. We stood next to the passenger side of the car and I began to tell him what had happened. I told him that first of all, his restaurant was a place I would avoid at all costs. When he asked me why, I told him my son and I ate there not a week ago, I told him how I had lost my adopted son, a son I raised as my own, a grown man whom I knew had his troubles, but to what extent... And I asked the Greek restaurant owner if I could, as a father, as the caretaker of the family, ever truly forgive myself. The Greek restaurant owner looked at me carefully for a while, then he put his hand on my shoulder and it was in that moment I noticed we were around the same age. We both had white-and-gray hair. I can tell you we were both very tired that day; the Greek restaurant owner had struggled to understand me because of the traffic noise. The Greek restaurant owner squeezed his hand on my shoulder and he told me he had three sons of his own, three sons who worked with him in the kitchen, in fact, he named the restaurant after them, the restaurant was called THREE SONS, and that the life he lived with his sons in the kitchen was one of incredible satisfaction and, at times, joyful. It was possible to find joy in that grind of a kitchen. And it would hurt him tremendously if one of his sons were to kill himself, especially given the life he had built for them, said my adoptive father. The restaurant owner looked me straight in the eye and said, I think you know what I mean when I say the life I've built for them, I think you're a man who can understand that. You seem to me like a man who would build a life for his children, the Greek restaurant owner said. It would be incredibly painful if one of my sons died like that, said the Greek restaurant owner, incredibly painful. His voice rose above the traffic and he started to yell, It would be incredibly painful! And then the Greek restaurant owner went on to say that it probably wasn't best to ask oneself the question of forgiveness a few days after the death, said my adoptive father, but I don't think I'll ever forgive myself. I didn't see it coming at all, I didn't see it coming… do you understand, Helen? I didn't see it coming… he said.

He reached out to touch my arm and began to weep again. I let him touch my arm even though I was very uncomfortable and did not know what to do.

Have you ever heard of the Waterfall Coping Strategy? I said. I could tell you about it some time if you want.

He stood up and handed me the keys and a wad of twenties.

The tank's full, he said. The morning of his suicide, some automobile specialists came and picked up the car. They took it somewhere and cleaned it all out. Then they dropped it off here. When I got into the car and sat in the driver's seat, it was like a brand-new car. It was like nothing had happened. It must have all been a dream. I tricked myself into thinking that. But I couldn't wake myself up. Then I knew it was real, it wasn't a dream or a nightmare. He's dead. My son is dead. The specialists told us it wasn't difficult to clean. In their estimation, they have cleaned up much worse. It wasn't that messy. He was always so careful!

I thought I was going to throw up. I started to retch, which caused my adoptive father to go to the door. Before he left, he told me the funeral would be at nine o'clock sharp, and that I didn't have to go if I didn't want to, that he and my adoptive mother would understand. We won't force you to go, he said.

That's exactly what Uncle Geoff said. Is he even my real uncle?

Uncle Geoff is your real uncle, sighed my adoptive father.

He shut the door firmly.

42

EVERYTHING LINED UP, I thought, everything planned, nothing decorative left, nothing on the computer except that one thing, *his death was of a beautiful design*. His hope must have been that the hospital would come as soon as possible to collect the organs and tissue-matter before things congealed and stopped working.

Compelled by my own sense of the ethical, I took the keys and money and went downstairs and into the kitchen, which was empty. I heard the water flow into and out of the pipes upstairs, everyone was showering and flushing. I helped myself to a slice of bread, untoasted. I had no choice, I, Sister Reliability, had to do this thing for my adoptive parents. It must have taken me half an hour to convince myself to go into the garage, and once in the garage, into his car, the site of his suicide. I saw a small version of myself above, watching my body slide into the black gleaming car, that terrible death machine!

You're doing fine! said the small version. Get in all the way!

His legs were much shorter than mine, so I spent a minute adjusting the seat. When I put the key into the ignition, the radio blasted on, a loud and aggressive heavy-metal song. Did he like heavy metal? Is this the music he listened to as he drove to the hospital? I shut it off. Whatever mess he left behind had been expertly wiped off and cleaned up, I said to myself, and they didn't bring it back until it looked and smelled brand-new.

When people like my adoptive brother come into your life, I thought, you are very lucky and, at the same time, very unfortunate. People like him can't be helped, because they don't want help, they are disgusted by our help. In the end, he had enough.

He once told me that he wanted good things for the people in his life, and for strangers.

If he had lived a little longer, he would have turned thirty.

Sitting in the driver's seat, I was astonished at how content I felt in that immaculately clean and artificially scented vehicle. It was his last place, I thought, and a real place of rest for him. Of course he killed himself in his car! Throughout my investigation, I had underestimated the power of his car as a meaningful object. He left it to my adoptive parents in sellable condition. He also attempted to leave his organs, his eyes, his tissues, his skin, his beautiful, immaculate skin to people who wanted to remain alive. And his skull did not blow apart, *because he was so careful*, the thinking organ extinguished in a matter of seconds.

I arrived at the drugstore. I told them I was there to pick something up for Paul and Mary Moran. It took the woman behind the counter a long time to find the package. She was a pleasant older lady, tall with long, bright white hair; I thought it was nice that she seemed to enjoy her job. She handed over a comically large envelope, almost the size of a door. I peeked into it, then I asked her if she knew him.

What do you mean? she said.

The person in the posters you developed, I said, did you recognize that person?

She told me she never pays attention to the content of whatever she develops; she focuses on the task at hand. I thanked her and left.

Back in his car, I opened the envelope and lifted out THREE HIDEOUS POSTERS of him, my adoptive brother, including what must have been the most recent photograph, the one from his birthday dinner, and also the photo from the department store, the picture with the three of them posed around the fireplace, only my adoptive mother's eyes were focused on the camera. The third and final picture was one I had never seen. It looked like it might have been from his high school graduation portfolio, he was dressed in his usual blue polo, posed in front of his brand-new car, kneeling down, hugging the family dog close to his chest. Both now dead, I thought. That poster was especially morbid. I understood that the posters were to be displayed prominently at the funeral, and then what would happen to them? Where would these posters go? I might offer to take one with me back to New York City, I thought, and set it up on my side of the shared studio apartment. I looked at the dashboard clock.

It was a bright sunny day, almost like the beginning of summer. The sun heated up the black vehicle quickly, causing me to sweat. The funeral was to start in half an hour, and instead of driving home or to the church, I saw a grocery store not a block away. I went in and picked out a large chocolate sheet cake for after the funeral. Set inside the grocery store was a little flower shop. I had some money left over from what my adoptive father gave me, and I decided I would use that money to buy new flowers, to replace the ones I had killed. I could even pitch in some of my own money, I thought. There was a gay man at the counter, and an older woman who was small with curly black hair and glasses that sat on the tip of her nose. They helped me select a wonderful and diverse arrangement of subtle flowers that I knew would do nothing but brighten and cheer up the drab and depressing ceremony. The brightness of the flowers would cancel out the dark and morbid poster display, I thought.

I pictured the people already beginning to stream into the church, my adoptive mother and father, the grief counselor at their side, standing near the altar, not on it, but near it, as people lined up to give them their condolences. I heard a few people, mostly parents of their own children, telling my adoptive parents not to blame themselves. I imagined people crying and giving my adoptive parents envelopes with cards. Of course, I would play the estranged adoptive daughter in distress. I would keep my mouth shut for a while. For a year. For a decade. For a life. The altar would appear somber and sparse without the posters and the flowers. Someone would play a fugue on the organ, perhaps Bach in B minor. The grief counselor would whisper to them terrible, brainless things about the invisible and cancerous tumors. There would be a dreadful service, notable only for its dreadfulness, nothing would take on meaning, the center would not hold. The priest would say many unremarkable things. A few young men, mostly my adoptive father's coworkers' sons, would carry the casket out to the hearse. After the service, my adoptive father would invite everyone to a luncheon in the basement, where everyone would devour my sheet cake. People would sit awkwardly at numerous card tables, and some people would come up to console me, to say how sorry they were, and then I would begin to ask them questions. I saw all of this very clearly and mercilessly.

We do whatever we have to do to keep ourselves from going into the abyss, I once listened to five hours of Fiona Apple albums to distract myself from the abyss, that itself is the abyss, I thought. My adoptive father had texted me the address of the church. I entered it into my phone. It was approximately thirty minutes away, on the edge of a bad neighborhood, far from the suburb they lived in. Of course my adoptive parents would go to a church with all the poor people. At the fifteen-minute mark, there were signs indicating a detour due to construction, which confused me. My phone went crazy, and the GPS failed to find a new route. I decided to ignore the detour, to just drive through the way I was routed originally, because I had no idea where the detour would lead me. So in the space of five minutes, I made a couple terrible decisions. How do we live with ourselves? I asked myself. There must be a way, but no one has ever told me.

TO LIVE AND LIVE ON, I shouted in the car.

Then everything turned slowly into a disaster, the street that I thought I was somewhat familiar with turned into a different street that led into a segregated part of the city, and ultimately ignoring the detour became the fatal error of the day, because as I drove through the bad part of town, the never-ending street with boarded-up houses and bricked-up windows, imagine my horror when the most perfect black car's tires bumped as if I had run over a small animal, then bumped again, as if the small animal had attached itself to the wheel, and then the entire car bounced up and down like a tiny sailboat in the middle of a hurricane, causing me to become nauseous, then the car itself sagged to the side.

I pulled over and got out of the car; it was clear that I had a flat tire on the worst possible day, at the most crucial moment, a true disaster. It was with great anxiety that I went back into the car and fished around the glove compartment for the car manual and tried to locate the directions for attaching the spare. I called my adoptive father and his phone rang. I called my adoptive mother and no one answered. I didn't have any relatives' or neighbors' numbers or I would have called them. Then, after fifteen minutes of attempting to remove the jack, I gave up. I realized the funeral must have started without me, without the posters, without the flowers. I felt worse than when I fell into the ditch, and almost as bad as when I received the phone call from Uncle Geoff. Devastated, I sat on the side of the street and stared at the flat tire. Sunshine streamed into the black car. The flowers wilted inside. The cake frosting melted and congealed. The posters became
9 *flattish and faded.*

43

IF SOMEONE ASKED ME to describe myself, I would say I was the adoptive sister who missed her adoptive brother's funeral. I, Sister Reliability, the most reliable one of them all, never showed up, I failed to make an appearance. People asked, Where is his sister? My adoptive parents were too busy greeting people to check their phones. My adoptive father assumed I decided not to go, and he told my adoptive mother not to worry about it. It was a terrible assumption. Of course everyone thought I was a hideous monster for not attending.

She thinks she's too good for his funeral, I heard them say.

Perhaps they interpreted my absence as disapproval of suicide, who can say?

I called five different taxi companies, and each time I gave them the address, the dispatcher hung up. Everything happened because of one bad turn. Everything bad went in a circle. It took hours for someone to come and tow the car, and once the car was towed, I started walking. I walked two miles in the heat through a bad part of town, wearing a black turtleneck and carrying the posters and cake and a few of the flowers, when a complete stranger picked me up and dropped me off at a gas station in a better part of town. By the time a real taxi picked me up and brought me to the church, the church was empty, the parking lot empty, nothing left but a great dry emptiness in front of me.

The day I was unable to attend my adoptive brother's funeral, I told the taxi to take me back to my childhood home. When I checked my phone, I noticed there was a message from my supervisor; I listened to it multiple times to make sure I understood correctly. My workplace investigation had been closed, and it was concluded that the results were inconclusive; the person who made the complaint changed her story too many times, she was unreliable, they couldn't trust her, and, besides, it wasn't right to investigate someone when they were going through such a difficult time, we're humans after all, he might have said, therefore, the investigation into my behavior and professionalism was dismissed. He told me how sorry he was for my loss, how he couldn't imagine what I was going through. He asked for the address of my adoptive parents' house and told me to keep my eyes out for a bouquet of flowers from an award-winning florist, he emphasized, and a card signed by everyone in the entire organization, even some of my favorite troubled young people. I had been validated, *the world* was inconclusive; and for no reason, I pictured my adoptive brother saluting me from his grave.

When I got home from the church, I encountered my adoptive mother sitting quietly with my aunt in the living room. My adoptive mother had a dreamy look on her face, as if she were outside of space and time. I asked her how the funeral went. She smiled and when I repeated the question the smile went away. What a stupid question, I thought. My adoptive brother was laughing from his omniscient perch. He's laughing at the entire situation.

I didn't go not because I didn't want to, I said to the two of them sitting on the wicker-basket couch, on the contrary, some terrible circumstances prevented me from being able to go. I'm sorry.

My adoptive mother and my aunt must have both been drinking all day, because my aunt looked at me blankly and said, That's a nice thing to say to your mother, Helen.

A few minutes later, the front door opened and I heard voices. A huge group of relatives and neighbors came in. They were talking about how the relatives who stayed in the upstairs bedrooms were poisoned, and had to be taken to the hospital. I wondered if they were talking about my childhood bedroom and the insecticide.

Is that what you're talking about? I said.

People looked at me, no one answered.

You would not believe how many people showed up, I heard them say, hundreds of people. The church was packed!

And to think another young man died in this neighborhood, said a relative. And so soon after this death.

Did you know he knew that many people? a neighbor said. Did anyone have any idea?

Someone hauled in case after case of boxed wine. I asked my cousin Fran about the location of the grave and he gave me a cemetery map and a funeral bulletin. My cousin Fran was closer to me in age than most of the relatives; he told me the cemetery closed at dusk, like most cemeteries, but I could probably sneak in somehow if I wanted to. I noticed the mass included "Amazing Grace" and not one fugue by Bach or anyone. The neighbors and relatives were gathering together to share a toast to my adoptive brother, which I thought was strange, since my adoptive brother never drank, and probably hated toasts, then they all decided to go to a movie, GRAVITY starring Sandra Bullock. They asked me if I wanted to come, but I couldn't answer, words left me. My adoptive parents went to bed at five in the evening. Everyone else went to the movie.

Inside my childhood closet I found a red canvas backpack from third grade, a time when one was excited about a new backpack because it was a backpack for high school or college students, it was especially sturdy and rugged and mature. Now the bottom of it was thin and worn down, the fabric see-through. I packed a flashlight, a Fiona Apple CD, the *Bitches Brew* record, and a box of cigarettes, stale old cigarettes that I stashed away inside a dusty bath mat when I was in high school. Guess what? The bath mat was still there.

I left the house and boarded the local bus. The bus ride took forever and I began to feel an everlasting peace. I must have been smiling, because a homeless man approached me.

Hey pretty girl, he said, what do you have for me?

It was nice to be called pretty for once, I thought, and I gave him a dollar. The bus dropped me off and I walked two miles to the auto mechanic, where I picked up my adoptive brother's car. I drove out to the cemetery in the dark listening to a Fiona

Apple CD, and smoking a disgusting cigarette, a shitty tube of death vapors. At the cemetery I squeezed through a gate to get inside. There were security lights up in the trees, and they made crazy shadows over everything; still, I could discern the shapes of trees and gravestones and flowers, and the mausoleums like little houses as I went toward the abyss.

I took out my flashlight. When I saw the small, self-effacing patch of dirt without a marker or stone or plaque or name or date or anything, I knew. I saw it so clearly, it was like looking into a shallow and ancient lake on a bright endless day. We had days like that in childhood, bright days that on the surface seemed endless, and each one ended, ended, ended, ended, and we were so bored throughout that time of bright endless days ending, we would have killed ourselves back then, if we had known it was a possibility to obliterate the self. But we were children and we were dumb. We didn't know anything. It was an adult solution, I thought, *his* adult solution. I saluted him back, my fucking dead adoptive brother! I didn't feel anything as I looked at the dirt, because I knew then exactly what he had done. When he killed himself, it was the first thing in his life he had ever done for himself, I thought, and the most generous thing he could do.

THANK YOU

My deepest thanks to Andi Winnette, a tremendous editor and kindred spirit. Thank you to the team at McSweeney's: Sunra Thompson, Ruby Perez, Claire Boyle, Kristina Kearns, Jordan Bass. Thank you to my incredible agent Kate Johnson and everyone at Wolf Literary. Thank you early readers Rita Bullwinkel, Rebecca Elliott, Dan Ivec, Jac Jemc, Jan Kruse, J, Brandon Shimoda, and Anne K. Yoder. Thank you Colin Winnette, Kurt Skaife, Bri Smith, Jes Seamans, Alyssa Tuma, the Riepenhoffs, Sarah Peck, Mikki Adamson, Claire Donato, Amina Cain, Rachel James, and Brandi Wells for friendship and inspiration. Thank you Fiona Apple for existing. Thank you Meridith for the deep love and support. Thank you to the Kruse family, Franny, and my parents for everything.

NOTES

CHAPTER 1

1. "Life itself is the instinct for growth, for survival, for an accumulation of forces...": Friedrich Nietzsche, *The Portable Nietzsche*, trans. Walter Kaufmann (New York: Penguin, 1977), 572.

CHAPTER 3

2. "Life was taking revenge on me": Clarice Lispector, translated by Idra Novey, from *The Passion According to G.H.*, copyright ©1964 by the Heirs of Clarice Lispector, translation copyright ©2012 by Idra Novey. Reprinted by permission of New Directions Publishing Corp.

CHAPTER 4

3. "His death, his death, a death that I abhor": William Shakespeare, *The Merry Wives of Windsor*, 1858.

CHAPTER 6

4. "hardly weltering, [died] away": William Wordsworth, "An Evening Walk Addressed to a Young Lady," 1787.

CHAPTER 10

5. "my thoughts began to burnish, sprout, and swell": George Herbert, "Jordan (II)," *The Temple*, 1633.

CHAPTER 13

6. "the leafy month of June": Samuel Taylor Coleridge, "The Rime of the Ancient Mariner," 1834.

CHAPTER 19

7. "deathward existence": Thomas Bernhard, *Correction*, trans. Sophie Wilkins (New York: Vintage, 2010), 141.

CHAPTER 37

8. "You too have weapons.": Franz Kafka, *The Diaries* 1910–1923, trans. Martin Greenberg, ed. Max Brod (New York: Schocken Books, 1976), 423.

CHAPTER 42

9 "flattish and faded": Vladimir Nabokov, *Lolita* (New York: Vintage, 1989), 305.

ABOUT THE AUTHOR

Patrick Cottrell was born in South Korea and grew up in Chicago, Pittsburgh, and Milwaukee.